PUFFIN BOOKS
VIKRAM AND VETAL

Poile Sengupta has written several books for children. Her published works include *The Exquisite Balance*, *The Way to My Friend's House*, *Story of the Road*, *How the Path Grew* (CBT), *Waterflowers* (Scholastic), *Role Call* and *Role Call Again* (Rupa). Her stories have appeared in various anthologies like *The Puffin Treasury of Modern Indian Stories*, *Sorry, Best Friend*, *One World* (Tulika), and *The Best of Target*. Her column, 'A Letter to You', ran in *Children's World* for nearly three decades.

Poile is also a playwright. She has written several plays for adults, of which *Mangalam* has been published by Seagull Books, Calcutta. She has also written one full-length musical and a number of short plays for children.

She has been a teacher at school and college and is a well-known theatre person in Bangalore, which is her home. Poile has recently moved to Delhi to be with her husband who is a senior civil servant.

VIKRAM
and
VETAL

POILE SENGUPTA

Illustrated by
DIPANKAR BHATTACHARYA

PUFFIN BOOKS

PUFFIN

Published by the Penguin Group

Penguin Books India Pvt. Ltd, 11 Community Centre, Panchsheel Park, New Delhi 110 017, India

Penguin Group (USA) Inc., 375 Hudson Street, New York, New York 10014, USA

Penguin Group (Canada), 90 Eglinton Avenue East, Suite 700, Toronto, M4P 2Y3 (a division of Pearson Penguin Canada Inc.)

Penguin Books Ltd, 80 Strand, London WC2R 0RL, England

Penguin Ireland, 25 St Stephen's Green, Dublin 2, Ireland (a division of Penguin Books Ltd)

Penguin Group (Australia), 250 Camberwell Road, Camberwell, Victoria 3124, Australia (a division of Pearson Australia Group Pty Ltd)

Penguin Group (NZ), cnr Airborne and Rosedale Roads, Albany, Auckland 1310, New Zealand (a division of Pearson New Zealand Ltd)

Penguin Group (South Africa) (Pty) Ltd, 24 Sturdee Avenue, Rosebank, Johannesburg 2196, South Africa

Penguin Books Ltd, Registered Offices: 80 Strand, London WC2R 0RL, England

First published in Puffin by Penguin Books India 2005

Text copyright © Poile Sengupta 2005
Illustrations copyright © Penguin Books India 2005

10 9 8 7 6 5 4 3 2 1

Typeset in Bembo by Mantra Virtual Services, New Delhi
Printed at Pauls Press, New Delhi

Contents

Introduction

The stories of King Vikramaditya and the Vetal are part of the classic tradition of Indian storytelling where serious social issues emerge from what are also engaging tales for children. There are many retold versions of the Vikram Vetal tales in our Indian languages but about twenty-five stories seem to form the original core. They range from the solemn to the comic and even the absurd, and most of them provoke serious questions about justice, governance, human behaviour and relationships, and focus strongly on the importance of plain common sense. This book retells thirteen of these stories.

The main narrator of this book is a girl whose otherwise boring summer holiday is suddenly transformed when she meets a strange storyteller. The girl's life entwines mysteriously with that of King

Vikramaditya's, and time and space lose their demarcations. By using a spunky and outspoken schoolgirl as the protagonist, the book pulls the age-old Vikram–Vetal tales forward into our own time. The girl's reflections help the reader discover the deep layer of meaning that each story offers even now.

Poile Sengupta

The Girl

He was an old, old man. So old that the skin of his hands looked like wrinkled parchment and he smelt peculiar. I could not see much more of him than his hands, because even in that high summer heat, he was completely covered in the folds of what looked like an ancient robe. My mother would have told me to stay clear of him. 'One never knows,' she would have said, 'one hears so many strange things.' My mother always hears vague, strange things that other people never seem to. But she was three thousand miles away, looking after my youngest aunt, who was about to have a baby, while I was spending my summer holidays here, at my grandmother's place. And I was angry and bored. What sort of holiday was this? My cousins were all busy with exams, or had some reason or the other for not coming. There was nobody to play with, no school tales to tell, no jokes to exchange. Instead, my grandmother was trying to teach me to cook and to stick to her rules, because, according to her, I was no longer a child. I was now a regular young lady. How I hated it. I hated learning to cook, I hated the rules. Most of all, I hated the waste of a whole summer holiday in that dismal, dusty town with no friends and nowhere to go, not even a library.

The old man was sitting under a huge tree whose branches spread out like the spokes of an umbrella. He was staring ahead, as if he was looking out at the sea, at sparkling white sailboats which were tracing disappearing patterns in the water, dipping and skimming, dipping and skimming like dancers on ice skates. All I saw was a deserted roadside with the heat shimmering like broken bits of glass.

'Sit!' his voice rang out suddenly. My skin jumped. How had he seen me when I had come up from behind?

'Sit,' he said again. 'Sit on the stone.'

What stone? I looked around and saw a grey, flat stone, under the tree. I touched it. It was dry, and curiously enough, it felt cool. I sat on it.

'Close your eyes and listen,' he said.

I closed my eyes. I waited. What was I supposed to hear?

'A story,' his voice said. 'A story that will serve you

well. Listen to it carefully. And remember, don't speak a word—not a word till I have finished.'

I had been brought up to be obedient and I can be obedient when I want to, though my mother would disagree. So I stayed quiet. He began. 'I call this story, "The Princess and the Three Kings",' he said.

The sun, high in the blue sky, seemed to dim as he began to tell his story. I smelt the green of dark trees, the moist earth, a dense black night. I was in a place that I didn't know and could hardly see. And yet I wasn't afraid. I had been here before.

'Once upon a time, there was a beautiful princess. When she grew up and it was time for her to marry, her father . . .'

The King

I am a king and, I think, a just king. At least that is
what my people say. The wise King Vikramaditya, they
call me, the good King Vikramaditya. The granaries in
my kingdom are bursting with grain, we are at peace
with our neighbours and the sweet rain falls when it
should, cooling the earth and the minds of men. Then
why am I, the fortunate king of such a kingdom, slashing
my way through this dark and dense forest, which sees
no light, either of the sun or of the fifteenth-day moon?
No wind visits here and no raindrops fall. Yet the earth
beneath my feet is cold and damp. It smells of dead
water, of things that rot even before they grow, it stinks
of never-ending decay. The darkness is an enemy, it
shows me shapes that are shadows and shadows that
are trees as thick as the walls of my fort. Large, hanging
rings of wet, sticky, furry leaves fall across my face and

around my neck as if they would strangle me, choke me, if they could. Nooses.

I cut them down, dozens of them, scores of them, and go deeper and deeper into the maddening darkness and into that smell that winds around me, entering my nose, my eyes, coil over coil. As I feel my way forward, I think of how I came to be here, far away from my court, my ministers, and my people. Far away from life.

It was the last hour of my public court, two new moons ago, when he appeared. He was a holy man. His face glowed, and his eyes pierced mine. He said nothing as he came up through the gallery of my ministers, not even his name. Then, when he reached me, he put his right hand into his robe and brought out a fruit and handed it to me. It was a strange fruit, golden-red like a mango but with a metallic smell. It lay heavy in my hands. When I looked up to thank him, he had gone. I put the strange fruit in the royal treasury because it was a gift for my people, not for me.

The next week, he appeared again just as before, and the next week and the week after. He said nothing, but each time he gave me one more of that strange fruit. Now there were four fruits in the treasury. When he came the fifth time, he spoke. He asked me what I had done with his gifts. I took him to the treasury, and there, to my astonishment, I found that each of those

fruits had turned into a gemstone of outstanding beauty.

The holy man smiled. 'I had heard you were a noble king,' he said. 'And now I know it is true. You alone can do what I wish.' He paused for a moment and then spoke again.

'In the middle of the dense forest at the edge of your kingdom, is a large tamarind tree. On one of its branches hangs a corpse. I want you to bring me that corpse. Remember, you have to do it alone, with no help from your soldiers. If you do this for me, your people will remain happy and prosperous for all time.'

Which king could resist such a promise? I took my decision without a moment's hesitation. I left the kingdom in the care of my ministers and began my quest. Now, here I am, slashing my way through a forest that seems to hate me, that wishes to slay me. I have to hold my courage close; I have to smell its fragrance. I am a warrior, nothing can defeat me, not even fear.

At last, I see it. The tamarind tree that he had described. It is large and broad, with many branches and thick foliage. In sinister light and shadow I search for the corpse, till I see it, halfway up the tree. I climb towards it. The tree sways and swings and heaves, I slip, I slither, but I will not let go. I grasp every branch I can reach, dig my feet into every hold and at last, I reach the corpse. It hangs limp like an old, discarded garment. I slide the blade of my sword beneath it and pick it off the branch. I place it over my shoulder and begin my climb down. My task is done, very nearly done. I merely have to go back the way I came and hand over the corpse to the holy man. My people will stay happy and prosperous for all time. That is what the holy man had promised.

Suddenly, there is a cackle of demented laughter, loud in my ears. 'What!' a voice says, 'You fool! You think your task is done?'

Who is it? Who is it that laughs? There is nobody here but the corpse and I.

'For someone so intelligent, you are strangely foolish,' says the voice. 'Did he not tell you about me? Your great sage?' The laughter rings out again, like the rattling of pebbles in a dry metal jug.

I look around, into what I can see of the tree branches, the wild grasses underfoot, the noose ropes hanging from above. There is no one.

'You cannot see me, you fool,' the voice cackles again. 'I am a Vetal.' And the entire forest with those great trees and beings of the night seems to take up the name and echo it: 'Vetal . . . Vetal . . . Vetal.'

'I am neither alive nor dead,' the voice continues. 'I have made my home in this corpse, but I am without life, without death, without rhythm. I am a Vetal.'

What does it want of me, this thing? It seems to read my mind.

'I want nothing from you,' it says. 'Nothing except silence. If you speak, if you utter a single word, I shall pluck this corpse from you instantly and take it back to its place. Do you understand?'

I am silent. The corpse hangs still over my shoulder. It is heavy, and cold and clammy to the touch. 'Then let us go on our way,' the voice says. 'Carry me to this great sage of yours.' I begin the long journey back through the slime and smell of the forest. My sword cuts down those clinging, deadly ropes that embrace my neck; it slashes through the heavy silence.

Then the voice is again in my ear. It is sweet now, like that of a friend. 'Great king!' it says. 'I too have heard of your infinite wisdom and your love of justice. I would like to tell you a story. You have to listen to it carefully. And remember, do not speak a word. Not a word.'

It starts telling the story. I do not want to listen. But I must. If I want to carry the corpse back to the holy man, I have to obey the Vetal. For the moment. 'I call this the story of "The Princess and the Three Kings",' the voice says.

The Princess and the Three Kings

Once upon a time, there was a beautiful princess. When she grew up and it was time for her to marry, her father, the king, invited young kings from all the neighbouring kingdoms to come to his court and try to win her hand. Her beauty and intelligence was well known and so the king's court became very crowded with hundreds of young kings, and a few old ones too, parading before the princess. Each of them had a herald who listed the qualities of the king as loudly as he could. One of the heralds boasted of his king's great wealth, another talked of how handsome his king was. One had a garden with the rarest of trees, another, an old one, was declared the best scholar in the whole world. Since many of the heralds did not stop speaking when they should have, there was a huge amount of noise, particularly when they started shouting at each other for interrupting. Finally, it became so bad that the princess said she had a headache and walked out of the courtroom.

There was an abrupt silence when she left and the competing kings wondered what was to happen next. They soon knew. The princess sent a message saying she liked only three of the kings who were assembled there and wanted to see them again. The others could go. There was great groaning and crying among the other kings but, as one of the more cheeky heralds said, how many husbands could the princess have?

The court was soon cleared and only the three kings whom the princess had named, remained. They were all very wealthy and powerful but each of them also had a special quality. One of them was an astrologer. He could read the stars, unravel secrets and discover hidden places. The second king was an inventor who had designed a clever chariot that could fly great distances at a tremendous speed. The third was a soldier. He was so skillful with his sword that people said his arm moved faster than lightning, faster even than a thought in your mind.

Whom would the princess choose?

'Let's stop for today,' said the king, her father to the three kings. 'The princess has gone to her rooms and my ears are still sore with all that shouting. Tonight, you three young men eat well and rest. Tomorrow when the sun rises, I shall ask the princess to meet you. She can make her choice then.'

So the three kings ate a good dinner, even though they must have felt nervous about the next day, and then had a good night's sleep. But the next day, much before the sun rose, they were woken up by a tremendous commotion in the princess's room. One of the princess's maids was wailing, another was screaming, a third was shrieking and fainting alternately. Surrounding them were the king's courtiers, jumping up and down and shouting, 'What has happened? Why are you wailing, screaming, shrieking and fainting alternately?'

It was only when the king arrived, his crown all crooked on his head and shouted at the maids, that everyone realized that the princess was missing. She had been kidnapped from her room in the middle of the night. Nobody knew who had taken her away.

What was to be done now?

'Don't worry,' said the astrologer king. 'I will find out who has done this terrible thing.' He closed his eyes, murmured a few strange-sounding words and said, 'A ferocious demon with many teeth has carried away our precious princess. He has imprisoned her in a dark cave thousands of miles from here. If we don't

rescue her within the next hour, he will eat her up for his breakfast.' There was a loud wave of crying and screaming from the princess's maids when they heard this. 'We will never see her again,' they wailed. 'Never. Never. Never.'

'Shut up,' snarled the king. Then he turned to the three young kings. 'Can't you help?'

'Yes, of course,' said the inventor king. 'Remember, I have designed a flying chariot. I can reach the princess immediately and rescue her. But I will need directions to the cave.'

'I will come with you,' said the astrologer king. 'I can show you where the demon's dark cave is.'

'Let me go with you too,' said the soldier king.

The other two kings were not very pleased at this suggestion. 'What can you do?' they asked. 'You are only a soldier.'

'You never know,' said the soldier king, 'I may be able to help.'

'Oh don't stand there arguing like politicians,' shouted the princess's father. 'Even now the demon's evil cooks may be looking up the recipe for roasting the princess in ginger–garlic sauce.'

So the three young kings, the astrologer, the inventor and the soldier, climbed into the fabulous flying chariot and sped away to the demon's dark cave. The demon smelt them as soon as the chariot touched the ground. 'Ha!' he growled. 'More breakfast. I want these fried. Fried kings in mustard was my mother's favourite recipe.' Then the demon lumbered out and smiled at the three kings, showing his many teeth. 'Come, my young fruits,' he said. 'Come into my kitchen, my fine cauliflowers.'

The astrologer king and the inventor king turned pale with fear, and they shook and trembled as the demon with his many teeth came closer and closer to them. But the soldier king strode forward and with a single, mighty swipe, he sliced off the demon's head with his glistening sword. 'Let us go into the cave now,' he said, 'and rescue the princess.'

In a very few minutes, the princess was rescued and brought safely back to the palace.

I had listened to the story in complete silence. The forest was hushed too, as if it had been listening to the story with me. Even the small, scampering invisible creatures at my feet were quiet.

'Now that you have listened to the story, will you answer a question?' asked my storyteller. I was silent. I had been told not to utter a word. So I would not.

The Vetal laughs into my ear. 'Now listen to my question,' he cackles. 'And if you know the answer, you better say it. Otherwise I will break your head into a thousand pieces. And what use is a king whose head is scattered all around this dark forest? The question is: which of the three kings did the princess choose to marry—the astrologer, the inventor or the soldier? Think! Which of them and why?'

'You have to answer the question,' the old man said. 'That is the rule. And the question is: which of the three kings would the princess have chosen to marry after she had heard what they did to rescue her?'

I thought for a moment. All three kings were worthy of the princess. The astrologer king had found out where the princess was imprisoned, and by whom. The inventor king's fabulous chariot had helped them reach the demon's dark cave. 'But it was the soldier king who actually rescued the princess,' I said. 'It was he who showed no fear and cut off the demon's head with a single swipe of his sword. If it wasn't for him, all of them, the three kings as well as the princess, would have been killed by the demon. I think the princess would have chosen to marry the soldier king.'

I speak. I have to speak although I know what will happen if I break my promise of silence. 'The answer is simple,' I tell the Vetal. 'The princess would have chosen to marry the soldier king.'

'Your answer is right,' screeches the Vetal. 'Your answer is absolutely right, great king. But you have broken your silence. You have spoken and I go back to my place on the tamarind tree. Here I go.'

The clammy weight has been taken off my shoulder and in the eerie half light, I see the corpse flying horizontally, arms hanging limply along its sides, back to the middle of the forest, to the branch high up on the tamarind tree where it had hung before. I follow it. I will not give up. No, I will not.

The sun was hot on my back and my arms were tingling. I opened my eyes. The shimmering field lay all around me but the old man had gone. It was as if he had never been there. Had I dreamt it all? I had listened to a strange story and answered a difficult question. How had I done that? The old man had been pleased. He had said, 'Your answer is right. Absolutely right.' But now when I wanted to ask him who he was, he had disappeared. There was no trace of him. I was completely alone in that field, sitting under a tree that looked like a gigantic umbrella.

I made my way home and to my grandmother's scolding. 'Haven't I told you not to wander about alone? Isn't there enough for me to worry about without your adding to it? Now let me see how clever you are. Make me a nice cup of tea.'

Does one need to be clever to make tea? Maybe, because when she tasted the tea, my grandmother spat it back into the cup. When I got up next morning, I found slips of paper pasted all over the door and on the mirror, which said in her scratchy handwriting: 'You must, must, must use only freshly boiled water when making tea.'

That evening, she had a visitor, an old school friend. 'Ah! There you are, dear,' my grandmother said smiling when I entered the room. 'This is my friend from school. We have known each other for almost three quarters of a century. Imagine that! I have just been telling her how well you make tea. Can you make us some tea and toast? You know where the toaster is, don't you?'

The tea turned out all right but the toast got all burnt on one side. I turned the slices over so that the better side was on top and served them. Then I murmured that I would have a bath, eat early and go to sleep. My grandmother was too busy talking to hear what I said. But I caught what she was saying angrily, as I turned to leave. 'Today's leaders,' she fumed, 'today's political leaders create monsters that they cannot control.'

Next morning there were more slips of paper stuck on my cupboard door and on the mirror. All of them said: 'You must, must, must check the settings of a gadget before you use it.' There was more scolding through the day and a lot of lectures from my grandmother on 'The Sensitivity of Old People and the Insensitivity of Youngsters' like me. Finally it was time for her afternoon bath and I ran out of the house to the brown, deserted field. He was there, the old man, sitting still as a statue, and looking out towards the far horizon.

'This is again a story about three people,' he said. 'I call it the tale of "The Three Sensitive Queens".'

I sat on the cool stone under the tree and closed my eyes. The forest wrapped itself around me like a damp, dark blanket. I listened.

The rasping voice is in my ear again as I climb down the tree with the dead weight on my shoulder and begin my walk across the forest. 'You don't give up, do you?' says the voice of the Vetal. 'You are very determined, aren't you? Speak great king, speak.'

I do not answer. I slash the deadly, swinging rings of vegetation with my sword. They seem to grow back almost immediately. But I walk on, shifting the corpse on my shoulder, so that it is not close to my face.

'Perhaps you are tired?' the voice goes on. 'I will tell you another story to cheer you up. This story is also about three people. It is the tale of "The Three Sensitive Queens".'

The Three Sensitive Queens

There were once three kings who were great friends. They had studied together at the same gurukul and their kingdoms were near each other as well. So whenever they could, the three kings met and feasted together and talked of the good old days, as men have done all through history. At these times, they would leave their queens at home saying they were going to be very busy discussing affairs of state. 'You know how it will be, darling,' they would say, 'all boring stuff.' Then they would rush out of their palaces, jump onto their horses and ride away furiously before the queens could ask any questions. Men have done this too, all through history.

Anyway, at one of these 'men only' feasts, the talk turned to how sensitive people can be. 'Especially queens,' said one of the kings. 'You should see my queen. She is so sensitive that she gives me heart attacks. I will tell you what happened just last evening. It is a strange story and you may not believe it, but it is true.

'Last evening,' the king continued, 'I was walking in the royal garden with my queen. I had a bit of a headache and I thought the walk would make me feel better. I was talking to the queen about the new digestive tablets that the royal physician had prescribed for me when suddenly she screamed and fell to the ground in a dead faint. You can imagine the shock to me. I too fell to the ground, screaming. Luckily, my royal attendant was close at hand, and he seems to have carried me to the royal bedchamber. He also summoned the royal physicians who treated me for shock and sudden stress.'

'What had happened to the queen?' asked one of the other kings.

'Ah yes, the queen,' said the first king, 'I had almost forgotten about her. But she is really the point of the story. When I recovered, I asked the royal physicians to examine her. Strangely enough, they had already done so, but even more strange is what they told me. They said that my queen had been very badly injured by a small white flower that had fallen on her left foot. It had hurt her so much that she had screamed in pain and fainted. I saw her injured foot with my own eyes.

It was red and swollen, the way my own foot had become once when I was much younger and got scratched by a thorny bush. Since then, on my orders, there are no thorny bushes in my entire kingdom . . . Where was I? Ah yes, the queen. She is conscious now but still in pain. Imagine getting so badly hurt by a small white flower! How delicate can a person be?'

The second king snorted. 'That's nothing,' he said. 'You should hear my story. Last evening, I too was with my precious queen, the rose of my heart. We were in the bedchamber, talking of this and that. I noticed how the moon had come out from behind the clouds and how the moonlight streamed into the room like a river of silver. I was just about to compare the loveliness of that delicate light with the peerless beauty of my own pearly moon when suddenly she screamed and fell into a faint.'

'Excuse me,' said the first king, who was not happy with the way his story had been received. 'Excuse me. Who screamed and fainted? The moon or . . .'

'My queen, of course,' replied the second king, impatient at being interrupted with such a silly question. 'My queen, my precious ruby, fell unconscious in my arms. I rang the bell furiously for her maids and for my attendants and for the physicians. They all gathered around, weeping and wailing. Then the physicians noticed that the porcelain skin of my rare diamond was covered with burn marks and blisters. I shouted at them. I asked how could such a thing happen, how dare such burns and blisters touch the skin of my treasure house. And then one of her maids pointed to the open window through which the moonlight was streaming in. Between sobs, she said that the queen could not bear the moonlight touching her. Her skin is so sensitive, that even the rays of that reckless moon cause her pain and give her burn blisters. Imagine that!

'My exquisite coral is able to recognize me now but it will take a week for her to recover. I have ordered that the windows of my palace be shut and curtained always and have directed my ministers to look for ways to keep the moon out of my kingdom altogether. That is how sensitive and delicate my unmatchable jewel is.'

There was a short silence and then the third king spoke. 'Don't know much about flowers and moonlight myself,' he said. 'Am a warrior, always will be a warrior. Tough, unbeatable. That's me. But the wife. She is different. Yes, sir. She is delicate. Yesterday, I sent for her. She was coming from her room towards mine. Suddenly she screamed and fainted right there in the corridor. Her hands were over her ears and those hands were covered with bruises. Have seen bruises sir, in the battlefield. But nothing like these. Nothing like these.

Sent for the physicians. They gave her a soothing drink. She opened her eyes. She said and I quote, "They are pounding rice. Oh, I can't bear it. Rice pounding." Unquote. Then she fainted again.'

'Was it some kind of delirium?' asked the second king.

The third king's face turned alarmingly red and purple by turn. 'Sir,' he roared. 'Mind your tongue. The wife is delicate, sensitive, not mad. She heard the pounding of rice in a commoner's courtyard, some ten crow miles away. She could not bear it. She covered her ears from the sound. She fainted. Her hands were badly, very badly bruised. The mere sound caused the bruising. Caused the faint. What do you say to that?'

The old man seemed to have finished telling the story. I thought of the three kings. Did they start fighting each other over whose queen was the most delicate and sensitive? Did they stop being friends? The old man's voice broke through my thoughts. 'The kings' activities are not relevant,' he said. 'You tell me which queen was the most sensitive.'

'Well, great king,' grates the voice of the Vetal in my ear, 'you are waiting for the question, aren't you? Aren't you?'

I do not say anything.

'Clever, clever king,' the voice rasps. 'This is the question. Which of these so-delicate queens was the most sensitive? I know you know the right answer. So say it. Say it, otherwise I will . . .'

'The third queen,' I say quickly. 'The third king's queen was the most sensitive. The other two were very delicate too but they fainted in pain when something actually touched their skin, a flower in one case, and the moonlight in the second. But the third queen fainted and her hands got bruised because of a distant sound. It was the mere sound of rice being pounded somewhere far away, that caused her such terrible pain.'

Even before I finish, the corpse has gone from my shoulder. I turn around and trudge back to the tamarind tree all over again.

'Your answer is absolutely right,' said the old man. 'The third queen was the most delicate.' I thought I heard him laugh, a sarcastic kind of laugh, but when I opened my eyes, he had gone.

When I reached home, I found my grandmother had gone out. She had left a note for me which said: 'Concentration is most, most, most important. Always concentrate on what you are doing, without thinking of anything else at that time. That is the way to success. P.S. I will be late today.'

For the first time since I met the old man I was alone at home and had the time to think of all that was happening to me. Who was this man? Why was he telling me these strange stories? How was he able to read my mind? Most important, how was I being able to give the right answer to his question each time? Suddenly I seemed to know the difference between right and wrong. It was as if I was someone else. My thoughts frightened me.

Next morning, my grandmother was busy. All through the day, she wrote letters. When the day got a bit cooler, she thrust the whole heap to me and asked me to post them. 'After that, you can go for a walk,' she said. 'You need some fresh air.' I looked at the envelopes. The addresses were all boring, office addresses. One was a lawyer's. I dropped the letters in the box and ran to the same dusty field that I now thought of as mine. He was there, the old man, his head turned towards the far horizon. I sat on the stone and waited for him to speak.

'This is the story of "A Comfort-loving King",' he said.

'He was not like you, this comfort-loving king,' the voice howls in my ear. 'Oh, he loved his silk and satin bedsheets and his perfumed clothes.'

The Comfort-loving King

The king liked his food served in golden bowls and he always ate off a gold plate. He loved the chink of the gold ladles and the way the light reflected on all the goldware. His palace was sprayed every morning with the scent of roses and every evening with jasmine. His ministers were not allowed to speak to him in court, they had to sing. And when he was tired, which happened every ten minutes, the ministers had to tell him funny stories while his attendants rubbed his feet with sandal oil. Yes, he loved comfort, this king, and he lived in great luxury.

One bright spring day, the king decided that he must travel to the woods at the edge of his kingdom. He had heard that it was a very pretty place, filled with flowers, and there was a delicate little stream brimming with beautiful fish that flowed through it. So he ordered his attendants and his cooks and his ministers to get ready and follow him to these woods. The air was fresh, his horse was strong and fast, so the king reached the woods much before anyone else. And then he got lost. He did not know whether to turn to the left or to the right, every tree looked like the next one. He was tired, he was hungry and his horse refused to carry him any more.

So our luxury-loving king wandered about the woods on foot, feeling more and more angry and hungry till he came upon the banks of the delicate little stream he had so wanted to see. And there, the king saw a hermit, sitting by the water, deep in prayer. Now, nobody, not even a king, should disturb anyone who is praying, but this king was so faint with hunger and tiredness that he went up to the hermit and fell at his feet, weeping. The hermit opened his eyes and muttered a few words. Suddenly, the king found himself in a bejewelled palace room, surrounded by platters of the most delicious food, served to him on a gold plate by maids who sang the names of the dishes that they offered. After he had eaten his fill, he was taken to a white satin and velvet bed, soft as the feathers of baby birds, where he slept the sleep of the satisfied.

But when he woke up, alas, the bed was gone, the palace was gone, and he was lying on the hard ground,

Vikram and Vetal

at the feet of the hermit who was once more lost in prayer. Again, the king showed no courtesy towards the hermit and began asking loudly, 'Was it all a dream? Was last night, so beautiful, so right, just a dream?'

The hermit opened his eyes. 'No,' he said, 'I created it.'

The king stared at the old hermit. 'You created it?' he asked in astonishment. 'You mean you have the power to create something so beautiful? You can do it at any time?'

'Yes,' said the hermit.

The king thought for a moment. Then he said, 'If you can, then I can too.'

'Certainly,' the hermit said. 'You merely have to develop your powers of concentration.'

'How do I do that?' asked the king.

'I will teach you the magic formula,' said the hermit. 'After you have learnt it, you will have to stand in the waters of this stream for forty days and forty nights and chant the formula without stop. Can you do that?'

'I will do anything to lead a life of comfort forever,' replied the king.

So he learnt the magic formula and stood in the stream for forty days and forty nights, chanting it without pause. The stream was cold, and at night it was even colder, yet the king did not give up. Alas, at the end of forty days and forty nights, when he tried to create a palace of luxury, nothing happened.

'Nothing happened,' he wailed aloud. 'I tested the formula, but I could not create anything.'

The hermit at the bank of the stream opened his eyes again. 'Prepare a ring of fire,' he said. 'Then stand in the middle of it, for forty days and forty nights, chanting the formula.'

Never in his life had the king done so much work. He dragged firewood and dry leaves and twigs to a small clearing in the forest. When he felt there was enough to last forty days and nights, he arranged the heap in a circle and stood in the middle of it. He then set the wood and leaves alight and began chanting the magic formula. The fire raged furiously around him, it made his eyes burn, it charred his hair, but he continued standing there in the terrible heat, chanting without stop. Then at last, he reached the end of the forty days and forty nights. He collapsed on the floor of the woods and again tested the formula. And again, he failed. No beautiful palace, no delicious food, nothing.

'No beautiful palace, no delicious food, nothing,' said the old man and stopped. I waited. Was this the end of

the story? 'That is the end of the story,' the old man said. 'But my question is, why is it that the king failed to create a palace of luxury for himself? He had done all that the hermit had asked him to do. He had learnt the formula, he had chanted it without stop, standing in the middle of a stream and then in the middle of a raging fire, for forty days and forty nights. But he couldn't get his palace. Why?'

'Why?' mocks the voice in my ear. 'Why did the poor king fail? Was the hermit making a fool of him? Answer, great king. If you know the answer, say it. Say it, or else I shall break your head into a hundred thousand pieces.'

I thought of the king and all the trouble he took to live a life of everlasting comfort. What were his thoughts when he did all those difficult things? Then I got the answer. The king was concentrating not on the magic formula he had learnt but on the palace and the food and the luxury he would get when he finished. Only his body felt the cold and the heat and suffered. His mind was on the rewards he would get. The hermit wanted the king to concentrate on the great power he had within himself, but the king thought only of comfort and how to pamper himself. As a result, he lost the chance to develop his inner qualities. He lost the chance to create.

'Excellent, great king, excellent,' grates the voice in my ear. 'But you have spoken and you know what will happen now.' The corpse is swept off my shoulder. I stop, I turn and make my way back to the tamarind tree. High above me, the dead man flies straight as an arrow, as if telling me the way.

'Excellent answer,' said the old man. 'Excellent!' His voice trailed away, and when I opened my eyes, he had disappeared. I walked back home slowly, thinking of all that had happened to me, of the stories I had heard—stories about a world I did not know, of kings and princesses, of strange magical powers. I thought of the forest that wrapped itself around me as the old man told me his stories; a damp, twilit forest that I had never seen in actual life but somehow seemed to know. I was not afraid of it.

'You are very deep in your thoughts today,' said my grandmother. 'You did not even notice me.' She had been standing at the gate of the house waving to me and I had not seen her. 'Come, come inside and have a good wash,' she said. 'Actually, you should have a bath.

That field where you sit every evening is very dusty.'

I almost tripped on the bathroom mat. How did she know? How much did she know? But when I came out of my bath, she was writing something furiously in a book. 'Eat,' she told me, without looking up, 'and then go to sleep.' I ate on my own, and thought of the many mysteries around me. Those stories. The old man. Now my grandmother.

'Good night,' she said when I had finished. 'Tomorrow I will teach you how to boil an egg.' Then, when I reached the door, she said something startling again. 'Do not think,' she said, 'that old people and blind people cannot see.'

I puzzled over that for a long time before I fell asleep.

The dead man's weight is on my shoulder again. I climb down the tamarind tree and begin the long, difficult walk back to the edge of the forest, where the holy man awaits me. Will I succeed this time? The Vetal has been quiet so far. I cut my way through the murderous rings of leaves. I test every shadow with my feet before I tread on it, I watch every tree before I go towards it. This forest has no kindness, it has the heart of a butcher.

'You are right,' the voice suddenly grates in my ear. 'This forest has the heart of a butcher. Talking of which, I want to tell you a story.' The Vetal's voice utters these words as if it has never told a story ever before. It speaks sweetly, innocently. 'This is a story of "An Old Man and His Blind Sons". And remember you are not to utter a word, not to open your mouth.'

The field was still hot, even though the sun was low in the sky. The tree above me sighed, as if it could not bear the heat. But the flat stone on which I sat was cool, and the old man wrapped in that black robe looked as if he did not even know that it was summer.

'This is a story called "An Old Man and His Blind Sons",' he said. I was so startled that I opened my eyes. The old man stopped. Then a moment later, he said, 'Please keep your eyes closed. And don't say a word.'

An Old Man and His Blind Sons

There was once a king who was known to be kind and generous to all those who came to him for help. One day, an old man came to the king's court, asking for a loan of five hundred gold coins. 'I am a carpenter, Your Majesty,' said the old man, 'and I have fallen on bad days. If you would kindly lend me five hundred gold coins, I promise I will return the money as soon as I set my business right again.'

'How do I know that you will not run away with the money?' asked the king who seemed to be clever as well as kind.

'That is why I have brought my sons here,' said the old man. 'They will stay with you and work for you till I return.'

The king looked at the two young men. He noticed that unlike most people who look around them avidly when they are in a king's palace, these two young men were staring straight ahead, their faces blank.

'How can two blind young men be of any use to me?' asked the king.

'Your Majesty,' replied the old man, 'my sons may not be able to see, but they have excellent sense of smell and touch. The older boy is an expert on horses, and his brother can assess gemstones better that any jeweller with the keenest eyesight.'

The king was more amused than believing, but he gave the old man the five hundred gold coins and agreed to employ the two young men in his palace.

A few days after the grateful old man had left, a horse trader came to sell a horse to the king. 'It is a magnificent horse, Your Majesty,' he told the king. 'A magnificent horse.' The trader always said everything twice, as if repetition added value.

The horse did indeed look magnificent as it stood there, tall and strong in the palace courtyard. 'A foreign breed, Your Majesty,' said the trader. 'A foreign breed. A very fast animal. A very fast animal.' The king wanted very much to buy the horse but he was not quite sure whether he should pay what the trader wanted. Suddenly, he remembered the old man's blind son who was supposed to be a horse expert. The king sent for him.

The blind young man listened carefully to the king and then went towards the horse. Very gently, he ran his fingers along the horse's back and down its legs. Now and then he smelt the body of the horse. When he came to the horse's knees, he stopped and felt them again carefully. Finally he said, 'Your Majesty, I would advise you not to buy this horse. It is a strong horse and can run extremely fast but it is unstable and will not allow anyone to ride it.'

The horse trader was furious. 'How can you listen to a blind man?' he asked. 'A blind man Is this any way to examine a horse? With fingers and nose? Fingers and nose?'

Nevertheless, the king decided to test the horse and sent for his best rider. But when the rider tried to mount the horse, it stood on its hind legs, whinnying loudly and shook him off. The rider tried again and again but the horse would not let him mount it. In fact, it threw the man off so violently that he fell on the ground and almost got trampled.

The king was extremely angry with the trader. 'You tried to cheat me,' he said. 'You were trying to sell me a killer horse.'

'No, Your Majesty,' cried the horse trader. 'No. The horse has never thrown me down. Never thrown me down. I swear. I swear.'

The blind young man laughed. 'This horse will not harm a milkman,' he said.

'A milkman?' asked the king and the trader together.

'A milkman?' repeated the trader.

'Your Majesty,' said the amazing young man, 'this horse is not of foreign breed. It seems to have been born in this man's stable. Its mother is probably an ordinary mare that this man uses to carry his milk pails. I could smell buffalo milk on the body of the horse. Maybe it has also been fed buffalo milk.'

By the time the young man had finished speaking, the horse trader had fled with his 'foreign bred' horse.

'Let him go,' laughed the king. 'That milkman will

not dare show his face here again. As for you,' he said
to the young man, 'you are truly a horse expert. Your
father spoke the truth and I shall never disbelieve him
again.'

So it was that when a jeweller came to sell the king
a very large and unusual ruby, the king sent for the
younger of the two brothers. 'Tell me what you can of
this,' he told him. The young man took the precious
gem in his hands and felt it all over with his fingers.

'Well,' said the king, 'what do you say?'

'It is a very valuable and unusual ruby, Your Majesty,'

replied the young man, 'but I advise you not to buy it.'

'What is your reason for saying this?' asked the king.

'It brings death with it,' said the young man. 'Every family that has owned the ruby has suffered disaster and untimely deaths. This jeweller himself lost his brother last week, a day after the ruby came into his possession.'

The king did not have to ask the jeweller whether the young man was right in what he said. Already, the jeweller had gathered back the ruby with trembling hands and was taking leave of the king.

Now the king was full of praise for the two young men. He boasted about them to his ministers and to his friends. 'So what if they are blind?' he kept saying. 'They can see much more than those who have sight. They are amazing. Truly amazing.'

After a few weeks, the old man, the father of the two young men, returned with the money he had borrowed from the king. The king was very pleased to see him. 'Your sons are marvellously talented,' he told the old man. 'Now tell me, since your sons are so gifted, you too must have some great talent yourself.'

The old man smiled shyly. 'Your Majesty,' he said. 'You are right. I do not have the unique powers that my sons possess, but I can tell the character and the family history of any man after taking only a single look at his face.'

The king sat back on his throne and said, 'Here, take a good look at my face and tell me something about myself. Who were my parents? What kind of man am I?'

The old man lifted his eyes and glanced swiftly at the king's face. Then he said, 'Your Majesty, you are the son of a butcher and you have a butcher's heart.'

The king jumped up from his throne, his eyes flaming red. 'Is that so?' he roared. 'Yes, you are right. I will show you how good a butcher I am. You and your sons will be put to death immediately.'

And so they were.

'And so, all three of them died,' rasps the voice in my ear. 'The old man and his two talented blind sons, all killed. Tell me, great king, who was responsible for their deaths?'

I stay quiet.

'You know the answer,' the voice is threatening now. 'If you don't say it, I will ...'

'The king did get them killed,' I say swiftly. 'Though he was generous, he acted like a butcher when he was angry. But he was not the cause of the deaths of the old man and his two sons.'

'So who was?'

I thought for another moment. 'The old man was himself the cause of the three deaths. He knew the true character of the king, but he did not have the wisdom to hide it. He told the king bluntly that he had the heart of a butcher. He was stupid and so he and his two sons died.'

The Vetal's voice comes from high above me. 'You are absolutely right,' it says. 'The father himself was responsible for the deaths. He was extremely foolish in telling the king his true nature. You are a man of great wisdom, noble king. But you have spoken and so I go. I go like the wind.'

I start again on the journey to bring down the body of the dead man. I begin my walk back to the tamarind tree.

My grandmother was sitting in the veranda fanning

herself, when I reached home. 'No electricity,' she said. 'You may as well sit here. It's cooler here than inside the house.'

I sat on a stool next to her and without thinking of what I was saying, I told her, 'You were right about blind people being able to see more than others sometimes. Actually, some people who can see are so stupid that they may as well be called blind.'

My grandmother stopped fanning herself and looked at me for so long that I felt uncomfortable. At last she said, 'I can see that you are finally growing up. I am pleased with you.' For a moment, she reminded me of the old man and his miserly words of praise. Then I shook myself out of that thought. This was not the strange, elusive, old man, this was my grandmother, my mother's mother whom I had known since I was a baby and who was trying to teach me to cook.

'Yes, I am pleased with you,' she said. 'And since you mentioned how stupid people can be, let me tell you a story. This is about a generous king and his far too loyal minister.'

'Can somebody be far too loyal?' I asked. Since my grandmother was telling the story I could ask questions.

'Yes,' she said and sighed. 'As I grow old, I realize that every human virtue has to be tempered with intelligence. Loyalty is good. So is salt. But one cannot have too much of either.'

The dead man is heavy and clammy on my shoulder. I climb down from the tamarind tree and start again on my journey back to the edge of the forest as I have done so many times already. 'Aren't you tired of this?' the voice is back in my ear. 'Why don't you give up? All you have to do is leave this corpse with me in it in peace and return to your beautiful kingdom.'

I do not reply.

The voice of the Vetal mocks me. 'You won't talk, uh?' it says. 'You are far too wary of me. Far too wary . . . so distrusting . . . Don't you know that even a good quality should be tempered? Let me tell you the story of "A Generous King and his Loyal Minister"—his far too loyal minister.'

A Generous King and His Loyal Minister

There was once a king who was a very generous man. He was so generous that his senior minister was worried there would soon not be enough money left in the treasury to run the kingdom and pay the salaries. He tried ever so often to talk to the king about managing his finances and saving for bad times. But the king only smiled and said that his kingdom would always be looked after.

One day, when the king gave away a large amount of money to a man who had clearly lost everything at cards, the minister felt he had had enough. He left the kingdom in the middle of the night and set off on a long pilgrimage. 'My king is a good, generous king,' he told himself. 'But really, generosity should also have some limit. One should not give everything away so that one is left begging on the roadside.'

The minister visited many holy places but his mind was always on the king. Finally, he reached a small village by the sea where he decided to stay for a while. Early one morning, before the sun had risen, as he walked along the deserted seashore, he saw something very unusual. He noticed that the waves a little distance away were turning colour, from blue-green to pink and orange. Suddenly, from among the dancing waves, a small island emerged, like a beautiful flower in a cluster of pink and orange leaves. There was a tree in the middle of the island that seemed to be made of gold; it shone so. Its branches were crusted with all sorts of sparkling jewels. And on one of these branches sat a beautiful girl, holding what looked like a handful of stars.

The minister stood on the seashore completely wonderstruck. He did not even think of the king for some time. And then, as he watched, the sun rose on the far horizon and the fabulous island sank into the depths of the sea and the waters closed over it. The waves turned blue-green again.

The minister stood for a long time on the seashore, thinking of what he had seen. The next morning, before the sun had risen, he was back at the seashore, gazing

out at the sea. And just like it had happened the day before, the waves turned colour from blue-green to pink and orange and out of the sea appeared a small, exquisite little island with a jewelled, golden tree and a beautiful girl holding a handful of stars.

This time, the minister did not stand on the seashore gazing at this fabulous sight. He waded into the sea and swam out to the island with powerful strokes. When he reached it, the beautiful girl jumped off the tree branch and helped him ashore. 'Oh, sir,' she said, 'you are completely wet. Are you a king, by any chance?'

The minister was taken by surprise. 'No, I'm not a king,' he said. 'Why are you looking for a king?'

'I've heard there are many kings in the human world,' the girl replied, 'and I do want to meet one. In any case, since you have got so completely wet all because you came to meet me, take these jewels and gold with you. I have lots and lots of it. Take it quickly before the sun comes up and I have to go back down.'

The minister gathered all that he could in his turban cloth, and then swam slowly back to the mainland, balancing the turbanful of treasure on his head. When he reached the shore and turned to look, the island had disappeared. The sun had risen.

The minister walked back to his rooms, thinking deeply of all that had happened. 'That strange, beautiful girl is looking for a king, for some reason,' he told himself. 'I have to return home. I have to go back to court and tell my king what I have seen and heard.'

So the minister set off as soon as he could to the palace, carrying those wondrous jewels and gold for his king. When he arrived at the palace, the king came hurrying forward to meet him. 'I have been so worried about you,' he said. 'Where have you been? What have you been doing?'

The minister asked to be taken to an inner room, where he told the king all that had happened and showed him the jewels and gold that he had been given. The king was very excited. 'This is just what I need for a charity that I have started. It is an old-age home for lame ducks,' he said. 'Come, let us give all this away and then go to that seashore.'

In a very short while, the king and the minister were on their way, and next morning, before the sun rose, they were at the seashore. 'Mind,' said the king, in a kingly sort of way, 'I will swim alone to the island and talk to this girl. You don't need to be with me. If I need you, I will call out to you.'

The minister got a little worried. 'But Your Majesty,' he said, 'suppose she is some kind of a demon in disguise. Suppose she were to harm you. How can I let you go alone?'

The king laughed. 'Don't forget kings are trained warriors,' he said. 'I can probably protect you better than you can protect me. But don't worry. I know I will come to no harm.'

Just as he finished speaking, the waves began to turn colour from blue-green to pink and orange, and from the depths of the sea rose the same sparkling little island, like a fresh, dewy lotus bud. The king stood transfixed for a moment. 'It is just as you described,' he said in a whisper. 'And she is so beautiful.'

The next minute, he had dived into the sea and was swimming quickly towards the island, while the minister stood alone and worried on the seashore.

My grandmother paused for a moment. 'What do you think will happen to the king?' she asked me. 'Will he be all right?'

'Oh please go on with the story,' I said to her. 'Don't stop now. I think the king will be fine. I'm not so sure about the minister though.'

My grandmother gave me a curious look and continued with the story.

The king reached the island and the beautiful girl helped him ashore, just as she had helped the minister. But this time, she took one look at the king and clapped her hands with joy. 'You are a king,' she said. 'You are a king. I know you are a king.'

'Yes, I am a king,' he replied, both amused and enchanted. 'What can I do for you?'

'You have to rescue me from an evil underwater demon,' the girl answered. 'Isn't that what kings do all the time?'

'Haven't done it recently,' said the king, 'but a rescue like this is described in Chapter 12 of the eleven-chapter textbook called *Training for Kings and Monarchs*. I even had to write an exam.'

'Oh goody good good!' exclaimed the girl. 'You only have to kill him and then my father and I will be free. My father has had a miserable time the last twelve years, laughing at all the demon's horrible jokes. That is our job—to laugh at his jokes. You can't imagine how horrid it has been. My poor mother died of boredom some years ago. Thank goodness my father is a bit deaf. I think that is what has saved him from certain death.'

'How have you managed?' the king asked, much concerned.

'Oh, by dreaming about a handsome, brave king,'

she said. 'I sit there dreaming and my father pinches my arm when I have to laugh. He says this is a very clever thing called Boardroom Strategy. It really works, you know. And oh, another thing before I forget, will you marry me after you have killed the demon and set us free? I do so want to be a queen and order the fish about.'

'Certainly,' said the king. 'I would like to marry you too.'

So the king quite forgot the minister and sank into the sea with the beautiful girl and the sparkling little island. The minister stood on the seashore dawn after dawn, waiting for the king to reappear. But he never did. He was so busy and happy under the sea that he forgot all about his old life. The minister waited for weeks and months and years. Then one day, he told himself, 'The king will not come back and people will say that I have done something to him. Who will believe my story? It is better that I die too.'

So he lay down on the seashore and died.

The Vetal pauses dramatically. 'So the minister died,' the voice in my ear says. 'Tell me great king, who was responsible for his death?'

I am silent. Why does this voice make me speak each time? Why does it make me break my promise of silence and the dead body flies back to that wretched tree? If I do not answer, I die. If I do, my work is never done.

'Speak!' commands the voice in my ear. 'Answer my question. Who was responsible for the minister's death? Speak, or else . . .'

I break my promise and answer. 'The king was not responsible for the minister's death.'

'Well,' said my grandmother. 'Can you tell me who was responsible for the minister's death?'

I thought for a while, sitting in that hot veranda with everything gasping for a whiff of wind. I thought of the dark forest that I visited so strangely when the old man started on his stories.

'I don't think the king was responsible,' I said finally. 'What was he supposed to do anyway? The minister introduced him to a wonderful life under the sea. So he stayed on there.'

My grandmother smiled a little smile. 'So?' she asked.

'Well, I think it was the minister himself who was responsible for his own death,' I said. 'Who asked him to run back to the king and tell him in secret about that island and the beautiful girl? Who asked him to take the king to the seashore without telling anybody else? Didn't he even think of the consequences?'

'Consequences!' my grandmother echoed the word. 'That is a big word to use.' Then she said, 'Everything we do has a consequence.' And then a little more softly, she added, 'What we don't do also has a consequence. And that was where Vikramaditya was caught. Between doing and not doing.'

'Vikramaditya?' I asked.

'The great King Vikramaditya,' she replied.

'You are right as always,' the voice of the Vetal screeches in my ear, 'You are right. The minister himself was responsible for his own death. But you have broken your promise great Vikramaditya, and you know the consequence of that. I go. I go and with me goes your prize. The body of a dead man.'

I turn around and begin to walk back to the tamarind tree. I find the ground yielding to my feet more easily now. How is that possible? It has not rained and yet the ground is softer than before. Then I realize that I have carved out my own path in this dark forest. My feet slip into my own footprints as I trudge to the tamarind tree and away from it and then back to it again.

'The great King Vikramaditya,' my grandmother said again. 'He trudged up and down a dark and dangerous forest carrying the stinking body of a dead man, all because he wanted his people to have peace and prosperity for all time.'

'But why should he carry the body of a dead man to get peace and prosperity?' I asked.

But my grandmother was already saying something else. 'His sense of justice has never been equalled,' she said, almost to herself. 'Look at the type of leaders we have now. All fools with egos as big as pumpkins. What do they know about justice?' She turned to me and asked again, fiercely, 'What do they know about justice?'

I didn't know what to say. I didn't even know what she was talking about. Her eyes were bright and hard like a knife and I was almost frightened. Then luckily for me, the lights came on and the maid appeared to ask what was to be cooked for dinner. My grandmother became my grandmother again.

After that, there were no more stories from her or strange, serious questions. She had no time for me. She rushed in and out of the house, carrying huge envelopes stuffed with papers and only had time to tell me to eat well and stay out of mischief. I didn't know what mischief she thought I would get into. What was happening was quite the opposite. I was actually being made to think about justice, the rule of law and of what is right and what is not. I had not done so much thinking in my life before. And certainly not during a summer holiday.

I ran to the field again, late in the afternoon. He was there, the old man, still looking out as if at a cool, serene sea that had cast a spell on him. Even before I could sit in my usual place, he had begun speaking. 'Now you will listen to a story called, "The Right Bridegroom for the Bride". There was once a man and his wife who had a very beautiful daughter. When the girl grew old enough . . .'

The corpse is heavy on my shoulder as I climb down the tree and begin my long walk towards the edge of the forest. My feet move almost without my knowledge, my sword makes a horrible sound as it slashes through the demonic ropes of leaves that come in my way. There is no other sound. There is no rasping voice in my ear.

No harsh laughter. What does this mean? Is the Vetal gone? Am I free? At last?

'Great king!' the voice is back, shrieking with laughter. 'I have gone nowhere. I am here. I watch your thoughts like a mother watches her child. Do you believe I can do that? Do you?'

I say nothing. Then abruptly, the voice is telling a tale. Another story. 'It is called "The Right Bridegroom for the Bride",' the voice grates in my ear. 'Say nothing. Just listen.'

The Right Bridegroom for the Bride

There was once a man and his wife who had a very beautiful daughter. When the girl grew old enough to marry, her parents looked about for a man worthy to be her husband. There were three young men in their neighbourhood who were brave, intelligent and good looking and who wanted very much to marry the beautiful girl. The problem was that neither the parents nor the girl could decide which of the three should be her bridegroom.

'They are all equally rich,' said the father. 'They all have lands and houses. And all three of them seem to be very good at managing their property. So our daughter will always be wealthy.'

'I have asked my friends,' said the mother, 'and everyone tells me that the three young men are also very hardworking.'

'And,' sighed the girl, 'they are all so handsome!'

This state of affairs went on for days and weeks and months. The three young men would visit the girl everyday, and several times a day, bringing her sweets and flowers and sometimes the poems they had written for her. The girl ate the sweets and tucked the flowers in her hair and read the poems. But she could not decide whom she liked the best. 'They are all so nice,' she told her parents. 'They all write such lovely things about how my smile is like a rainbow and my hair is as black as the sky without a moon. How can I choose? How can I?'

Then one evening, as the girl was walking about in the garden, thinking about the three young men, something terrible happened. A snake came out of the bushes and bit her. She screamed in fright, fell to the ground and died. When her father and mother found her dead, they were so heartbroken that they too died. As for the three young men, they were grief-stricken, and their wails and sobs could be heard all over the village that entire night.

But what was to be done? Their beloved was gone. After her cremation, the first young man took a handful of her ashes and floated them down the river. He gave up all his work, and sat alone by the riverside all day and all night long. The second young man collected the rest of the girl's ashes in an urn and started living in a small hut by the river, with the urn beside him all day and all night long. The third young man decided to travel as far as he could go, to get over his great sadness.

Months passed. One evening, the third young man, the traveller, was walking by a cottage in a village lane, when he saw something extraordinary. There was a small fire burning by the side of the house with cooking pots around it. Suddenly, a child came out of the house and ran towards the fire. His mother rushed out to stop him, but before she could reach him, he fell into the fire and was burnt to death. The young man watched in horror as the woman ran about screaming for help. Then very calmly, a bearded man came out of the cottage and walked up to the fire. He chanted a few verses over the ashes of the child and sprinkled some drops of water. Immediately, the ashes disappeared and the child jumped up, alive and laughing as if nothing had happened to him.

The young man realized that if he learnt the holy verses, he would be able to bring to life the girl he loved so dearly. So he introduced himself to the bearded man and asked if he could learn the verses. The bearded man agreed, and the traveller spent the night in the cottage eating a good dinner and learning the powerful

life-giving verses. Next morning, after thanking the good people who had helped him so much, he travelled back to his village, as fast as he could. He went straight to the riverside where he met the other two young men and told them what he had learnt. They were as excited as he was. Quickly, they brought out the ashes in the urn and spread them on the ground. The third young man stood for a few minutes with his eyes closed and then chanted the holy verses that he had learnt. The first young man sprinkled a few drops of river water on the ashes. And suddenly, the ashes disappeared and the beautiful girl whom they all loved, stood before them, as fresh and lovely as she was before.

The Vetal finishes the story and is silent. But I know what the question will be even before I am asked. 'So you know the question, is it great king?' rasps the voice. 'Do you think I want to know the holy words the young man learnt?'

I do not answer. I know no holy verses, no powerful words. I know only the words of justice, I can tell what is right and what is not.

The Vetal's voice rasps into my ear. 'So you know what is right and what is not? Is that so, great king?

Then let me tell you another story. And you can answer the questions to both stories together. Will you still remember this story, huh? Will you? Will you?'

I continue walking. If this second story is a long one, perhaps I would reach the holy man before I need to answer the questions.

'It is a very short story, king,' says the voice. 'A really short story. And again, it is about a girl's choice of a marriage partner. It is called "A Wise Decision".'

The old man stopped for a moment. I knew what the question would be though I was not sure of the answer. But instead of asking me the question, the old man said, 'Let me tell you another tale which is also about the choice of a marriage partner. But you will have to remember this first one because I will ask the questions to both stories together. The second story I am about to tell you is called "A Wise Decision".'

A Wise Decision

There was once a king who had a beautiful daughter. When it was time for her to marry, the king, like any father anywhere in the world, went about looking for the perfect bridegroom. He finally settled on four noble kings, all of whom, he thought, were worthy of marrying his beautiful daughter. The problem of course was, which of the four was the most worthy?

He decided to consult his queen. 'My dear,' he told her. 'They are all four very worthy men. The king from the east is an extremely learned young man. He claims he knows the deepest truths and can even bring the dead back to life.'

'Does he have money?' the queen asked.

'All four of them are very, very wealthy,' the king said, a bit stiffly. 'Don't you think I would have looked at that aspect?'

The queen smiled. 'What about the other three kings? Tell me about them,' she said.

'Well, the king from the west is excellent at managing his wealth. He knows how best to use his money productively.'

'Does he come from a good family?' asked the queen.

'Of course,' said the king in an irritated way. 'All of them are from very good families. Otherwise do you think I would have considered them at all?'

'Certainly not,' said the queen smiling. 'Please go on.'

'The third young man, the king from the south, is famous as a great warrior,' said the king. 'He is believed to be highly skilled in all the martial arts like swordplay and single combat and . . . many other things.'

'Is he handsome?' asked the queen.

The king was really angry this time. He threw down his notes.

'Why, my dear queen, are you asking me such stupid questions?' he shouted. 'Do you or don't you trust my judgement?'

'Of course, I do,' said the queen softly. 'I was just trying to make sure that the four you have chosen are all wealthy, handsome and come from good families. Please do go on. I promise I won't ask any more stupid questions.'

The king picked up his notes, and gruffly said, 'They are all very handsome. Anyway, there's not much more to tell. The last king, the one from the north, is extremely hardworking and is busy from morning to night keeping his people happy. There you are! These are the four kings that I think are worthy of our daughter. But the problem is, who among them is the most worthy?'

There was a small silence. Then the queen said, 'My king! You have chosen four excellent young men. But I don't see any problem in deciding which one of them our darling should marry.'

'You mean you can decide who is the best?' asked the king, cheering up considerably.

'You and I will decide on that together,' said the queen. 'First, may I ask you to look at the four young men from a slightly different point of view?'

'Yes, of course, my dear,' said the king.

So the queen explained to the king what she had in mind and he was very pleased.

'That's right,' he said. 'That is exactly what I think too. Yes, he really is the right choice. No question about it. I had come to that conclusion myself, long ago. Come my love, let us go and tell our darling daughter of my decision. I think it is a wise one.'

The queen smiled.

'So there you are,' says the voice heavily in my ear, 'In the first story, which of the three men should the girl marry? The first one who floated her ashes in the waters of the river or the second one who collected her ashes in an urn and sat mourning by it? Or should she marry the third young man who gave her life again? And in the second story, which of the four kings should the princess marry? Which one? Which one?'

The forest echoes with the question. Which one? Which one? Which one?

I had to think for some time before I could answer the question. It struck me that in the first story, the three young men did different things after the girl died. The first young man did what my father had done when my grandfather died. He took a handful of the ashes and floated them down the river. That is what a son does, so the first young man behaved like a son. The young man who brought the girl back to life did something wonderful. He made her alive again. But giving life is something that a parent does. This young man was therefore like a father to the girl. So it was the second young man, the one who mourned over her ashes, who was the most suitable of the three, to marry the girl.

'Excellent answer,' the old man said. 'Excellent! Excellent! And in the second story, which of the three kings should the princess marry?'

'And your answer to the second question, great king?' grates the voice in my ear.

This one is easy to answer. 'The princess should marry the king from the south, the warrior king,' I tell the voice. 'The others are all worthy men, but unsuitable for her. The warrior will protect her and his kingdom too. So he is the right choice.'

'Both answers are right, great king,' the voice of the Vetal says, 'They are excellent, logical answers, But you have spoken and you shall pay the price. I carry off what you so desire. I take it away.'

The clammy weight is off my shoulder again and I am forced to retrace my steps as I have done so many, many times since I entered the forest.

'Yes,' said the old man. 'Your second answer too is absolutely right and logical. A princess must marry a man who can protect her and his kingdom. That is the first duty of a king. Protection.'

Was this the right time for me to ask my questions? Now, when he seemed pleased with my answers? Surely I could ask him who Vikramaditya was and why he carried the body of a dead man and why . . . But when I opened my eyes, the old man was gone.

My grandmother was at home when I returned. I was hoping that she would be able to answer some of the questions that were biting me like persistent mosquitoes. But she was on the phone and clearly in a bad temper. 'What do you mean he has rights over the property?' she was shouting. 'Who looked after the old man? The son? Or the daughter? She gave up her studies to stay at home and look after him. What? Yes, I know that. But look, there are legal rights and there are moral rights. Yes. That's what I feel. Yes. Put it to him that if he wants all his father's money, he also takes on the responsibility of his sister till she gets married.' She banged down the phone and glared at me. 'Remember,' she told me, 'rights and duties are both six-letter words that mean the same thing.' She then went into her room and shut the door.

I don't know when she had dinner that night. I

kept feeling that in some strange way she was telling me to find the answers to my questions myself. I remembered my father saying to me once when I asked him to help me with some maths homework, 'If you don't work out the answer yourself, you will never understand it. Nor remember it.'

The heat was still blistering when I went to the field the next day. But I felt a softening in the air, as if somewhere far away there were dark clouds that were about to journey this way. The old man gestured to me to sit and immediately started on the story of the day. 'A story called "The Real Father",' he said. Then he paused. 'I think I shall start this story with a strange dream that a man once had,' he said.

How many more times do I go back to the tamarind tree to carry down the corpse? How many more times will the voice of the Vetal command me to answer questions, threatening me with death if I did not? How much more of this?

'But you always answer so well!' howls the voice high above me. 'Your sense of justice is incomparable. You are a king without a grain of arrogance or pride. You do not even look for comfort. Indeed, you are a remarkable man.'

The praise is empty of meaning. I can think of nothing but having to carry this dead body to the holy man waiting for me at the edge of the forest. 'Not yet, not yet,' rasps the voice. 'You have much more to teach the world. I will not let you go so easily, Vikramaditya. I have you in my power now and I will not let you go.' Then in a softer voice, he says, 'Let me make you feel better. I shall tell you a story. My story is called "The Real Father". Listen carefully, great king, as you always do. I shall start this story with a strange dream that a man once had.'

The Real Father

The man who had the dream was a fine wealthy young man whose father died suddenly one day, without any apparent illness. The young man had no mother and he cried bitterly on the day of his father's funeral, thinking how completely alone he was in the world now. But he was also a brave young man with a practical mind and so, after the funeral, he wiped his eyes and decided he would travel to the holy river in the next town. 'If I pray on the banks of the river,' he told himself, 'and give an offering of rice and flowers to the memory of my parents, I am sure I will feel better.'

So the young man prepared for the journey to the next town. But on the night before he was to travel, he had a strange dream. He dreamt that he was praying on the banks of the river, ready with his offerings of rice and flowers, when suddenly, from the water, rose three pairs of hands with outstretched palms. *Three pairs of hands.* The young man noticed that one pair wore bangles. 'That must be my mother,' he told himself. 'The other two are men's hands. But why are there two? There should be only one pair of hands, those of my father's. What is the meaning of this?'

The young man woke up with the dream still strong in his mind. 'I cannot understand why there were two pairs of men's hands,' he kept saying to himself. 'Why were there two?' Finally, he decided to go and see the wise man of his town and ask him for the meaning of the strange dream. 'There is no use my going to the river without finding out what this dream means,' he told himself.

The wise man lived in a small house in the middle of the town. He was a carpenter and a busy man. But when he heard what the young man had to say, he stopped his hammering and went out into the quiet of the courtyard. 'Sit down next to me and tell me about your dream again,' he said. The young man sat down and told him about his strange dream. When he finished, the wise man was silent for a few moments. Then he said, 'I have a story to tell you. And don't speak till I have finished. If you do, I will refuse to say another word. This is the story. There was once a poor man who lived with his wife and daughter in a hut at the edge of a town. The family just about earned enough to eat a meal a day but sometimes did not manage even that. One night, after her parents had fallen asleep, the daughter sat in front of the hut, trying not to think of how hungry she was. Suddenly, she saw the shadow of a man creeping towards her. She was about to cry out loud when he whispered, "Please. Don't shout. I need your help." She then noticed that his left arm was bleeding and his face was badly hurt. "Come inside," she whispered. "But you have to be very quiet, for my parents are asleep."

'The young woman took the man inside and helped him wash his face and the wound on his arm. "I have no medicines here," she told him. "This is all I can do."

'"I do not need medicines," the man said. "But I have one more favour to ask of you. You have to give me shelter for the night, but nobody should know I am here."

'The young woman silently showed him to a sagging old cot and herself lay down on the ground in the courtyard. Just as she was falling asleep, she heard shouts and saw several soldiers with lights running about here and there. Two of these soldiers came up to her and spoke to her roughly, asking her whether she had seen any strange man lurking around.

'"He's a bad man, a thief," one of them said.

'"He is dangerous," the other said.

'The young woman yawned and said she had seen nobody. "Now please let me sleep," she told the soldiers. "I have to get up early and wash the courtyard."

'The soldiers went off grumbling, saying it was all very well for her, she could sleep but they had to be up all night, searching for a stupid thief.

'"Why can't thieves rob during the day?" they said to each other. "Do they have to steal at night so that decent people like us are robbed of our sleep?"

'Next morning, the young woman got up early and let herself into the house quietly. But the stranger was already awake. He was sitting on the floor in the middle of a great spread of food and sweets and gold—lots and lots of gold.

'"This is all for you," he told the young woman who was standing at the door gaping at him. "You saved my life last night. Now I better leave before the soldiers return."

'The young woman did not move from the door. "You can't go," she said. "Your wound is still to heal and the soldiers won't come back. They are far too lazy."

'So the man stayed on. He met the parents of the young woman and after about a week, he asked them whether he could marry their daughter. They agreed happily. So the thief and the young woman were married. Soon, they all moved to a bigger house and began to enjoy their new life. But after about a year, the man said, "I am tired of sitting idle like this inside the house all the time. I'm sure the soldiers have stopped looking for me. Let me go to the next town and look for some work. We can't live on stolen gold all our life."

'Although the young woman and her parents were not happy with his plan, they let him go. What could they do? When a man decides on something, nothing and nobody can stop him. He went away for many months and in the meanwhile, his young wife had a beautiful baby boy. The baby began to grow up but there was still no news from his father—none at all. The family grew more and more worried and finally, the young woman's father decided to find out what had happened. He travelled to the next town. There he was told that his daughter's husband had been caught by the soldiers soon after he arrived there, and been killed.

'There was great grief in the house when he returned with the sad news. The mother of the young woman fainted and the next-door neighbour had to be called for help. This neighbour was a kind young man who had just moved to the town. He lived on his own and the young woman and her parents had often invited him to share a meal with them. It was now his turn to help them. The family certainly needed help because the old parents were so overcome with grief that they soon fell seriously ill and died. The young woman and her little boy were all alone in the world. What were they to do? How would they live? When the kind neighbour saw their plight, he offered to marry the young woman and help her raise the little boy. The woman agreed. But soon after they were married, she too fell ill and died. And so, the little boy grew up in the care of his stepfather, who he always thought was his real father. Nobody had told him the history of the family.

'The little boy grew up into a fine young man who became wealthy through hard work and intelligence. When he was about twenty-five years old, his stepfather also died. The young man cried bitterly on the day of the funeral. He had loved his stepfather very much and now he felt he had nobody in the world to love him. Then he decided to travel to the banks of the holy river in the next town and offer food and flowers to the memory of his parents. "If I pray and give offerings," he told himself, "I will feel better."

'The young man started to prepare for his journey,

but on the night before he was to travel, he had a strange dream . . .'

'Stop,' said the young man who had been listening silently all this while. 'This is my story and you are saying that my father was really my stepfather.'

The wise man nodded his head.

'But he took such good care of me,' said the young man. 'He loved me so much even though I was not his own son!'

The wise man nodded his head again.

'Then who is my real father?' asked the young man feeling as if he was lost in a dark tunnel of thought. 'Whom do I give my offerings to?'

But the wise man only smiled and went back to his work.

'The wise man did not answer,' cackles the Vetal's voice in my ear. 'He refused to speak. But great king, I am sure you know the answer. Who is the boy's real father? The man who was responsible for his birth? Or the man who brought him up so lovingly?'

'Who is the real father?' asked the old man. 'The man whom his mother first married? Or the man who took care of him and brought him up?'

I did not even need to think very much. I knew the answer. I knew who the real father was. It had to be the man who brought him up, the one who loved the little boy as his own child and helped him grow up into a fine young man. This was the real father. This was the man he had to give his offerings to, there was no doubt about it.

'You are right, great king,' grates the voice. 'You are absolutely right as always. In this case, it is not the actual father but the man who brought up the child, who is the real father. Absolutely right, noble king. But I am off. I am off to my tree. Off!'

The voice is high above me as I turn and make my way back to that wretched tamarind tree where the corpse hangs, as if it has never been moved.

'Yes, you are right,' said the old man. 'You are absolutely right.'

'But did the young man find the answer? Did he give his offerings to his real father?' I asked.

There was no reply. When I opened my eyes, there was nobody around. The old man was gone.

I went back home with questions buzzing around in my head. Was there nobody to give me the answers? The young man in the story must have felt the same way. What would he have done, I wondered. Then I remembered that he was much older than me, and he was supposed to have been intelligent. So he would have known what to do. He would have worked it out for himself.

But what I wanted was information. Who was this King Vikramaditya whom my grandmother had mentioned? I felt that if I got the answer to that question, the rest of it would become clear—the old man . . . the stories he told me . . . his questions. And the strange way I could answer those questions. How was I being able to do that?

Yes, I had heard of a certain King Vikramaditya. I had heard stories about his great sense of justice and of his bravery in battle. But when I looked through my history book, I found that there were several King Vikramadityas in ancient Indian history. It seemed to have been quite a popular name in those days. My mother had once said that people often named their children after some great person, hoping that their child would be great too. I wished that the mothers of the many King Vikramadityas had not thought the same way. Now I did not know which Vikramaditya carried the body of a dead man up and down a forest, so that his kingdom would be peaceful and prosperous. It seemed to me a stupid thing to do.

I stayed up half the night reading the entire history book. I did not even leave out the chapters on modern Indian history when all the kings had given up their titles for democracy. But I had not found my grandmother's King Vikramaditya.

I was back at the field the next afternoon and the old man's voice broke into my thoughts. 'Today's story is called "The Right to Property". Listen to it carefully.'

Rights? Duties?

'So we are back again on the same path are we?' the voice of the Vetal mocks me. 'You never do give up, do you? And for what? For what, great king?'

I will not answer. I slash my way through the infernal forest, where things never seem to die. Where things never seem to live either.

'Today I want to tell you a story called "The Right to Property",' the voice says. 'Listen carefully, great and noble king, listen to it carefully.'

The Right to Property

There once lived two brothers who loved each other very much. They stayed in the same house and worked together in a garment shop which their father had started. The two brothers were so good at their work that the business prospered and they often wished that their parents were alive to share in their wealth and good fortune.

It so happened once, that the two brothers had to go to the next town on some business. They wished to return home the same night so they tried to hurry with their work; even so, it was late evening when they finished. They were a little worried about travelling at night, because they had to cross a rather dark, wooded area to reach home.

'We might meet wild animals,' said the younger brother.

'Or thieves,' said the older one.

'But we could carry lights.'

'And talk loudly to each other.'

So in the end, that's what they did. They carried a great many bright lights and talked loudly and cheerfully to each other as they made their way through the woods.

'Our discussion on the king's taxes will scare away all the wild animals,' said the younger brother.

'And if I start singing my favourite lullaby, any self-respecting thief will run for his life,' laughed the older brother.

They were almost at the edge of the forest and their throats were just a bit sore with all their talking and singing, when they suddenly heard a strange sound.

'Like someone crying,' said the younger brother.

'Like a woman crying,' said the older brother.

Without another word, they went towards the sound and saw that it was indeed a woman sitting under a tree and sobbing her heart out. The two brothers were a little embarrassed.

'Could be a private matter,' whispered the younger brother.

'Maybe we should not interfere,' said the older brother very softly.

'But how do we leave her alone here?' asked the younger brother.

'The night is dark and the woods are deep,' whispered the older one.

So they coughed and sneezed and the older brother even snored, to catch the attention of the woman. Finally, when they were just about to sing, she looked up and saw them. 'Oh, sirs!' she wailed. 'Please help me.'

'Certainly,' said the younger brother, and realized that the woman was very young.

'Definitely,' said the older brother who noticed that the woman was very pretty.

'Oh, sirs,' the woman said. 'Nobody has said such kind words to me for a long time.'

'For how long?' asked the younger brother.

'Why?' asked the older one.

'Since this morning,' she replied. 'I was travelling with my brother when some thieves attacked us and my brother was killed and the thieves took away all my jewels and now I don't have anywhere to go and nobody to be with.'

'All this happened this morning?' asked the younger brother.

'You must be very scared and hungry,' said the older one.

'Yes,' the woman said. 'And indeed, yes.'

The two brothers stood a little away from the woman and had a short whispered discussion.

'I think we should escort her to the king's palace and leave her there,' said the younger brother.

'I think we should give her something to eat,' said the older brother.

'She can try and get some work in the palace,' said the younger one.

'She can then have a bath and feel fresh.'

'She will be a good queen's maid.'

'She will be a good wife.'

'She can . . . What did you say?'

'Her eyes are like stars. And I'm sure she cooks like an angel.'

The younger brother looked at his older brother and asked, 'Are you sure?'

The older brother nodded.

So they went up to the woman and the younger brother asked her, 'Would you be willing to marry my brother?'

The woman looked at the older brother and said, 'Yes. I would like that very much.'

By then, the first pink rays of the sun were already slanting across the eastern sky and the three of them came out of the woods easily enough. The younger brother immediately started making arrangements for the wedding while the older brother wrote rhyming poems.

'Do you want two types of sweets for the wedding or three?' asked the younger brother.

'She is my burfi, she is my rabri;

When she is here, what more for me?' replied the older brother.

At another time, the younger brother wanted to know what kind of clothes his brother would wear for the wedding. 'Do you want to wear silk or satin?' he asked.

'Her hair is like silk, her skin is satin,

When she is near, I speak in Latin,' said the older brother.

'What do you mean you speak in Latin?' the younger brother asked. 'You don't know a word of that language.'

'That's true,' replied the older one. 'But I can't find any other rhyming word for "satin". Can you?'

Anyway, the wedding was a splendid affair. The king was there to wish the couple and the food was delicious. All the townspeople said how pretty the bride was and how happy the bridegroom, and how tired the younger brother looked. Some of them asked the younger brother, 'So are you all going to live together?'

'No,' he replied. 'Our father had built two houses, next to each other. So far, one of them was all locked up, but I have opened it and cleaned it up and my brother and his wife will be living there.'

'Very sensible, very sensible,' said the townspeople, and had more helpings of the delicious food.

So the older brother and his bride moved into the other house, and after about a month, the man stopped writing poetry and came back to work.

'I think it is better that we divide up the business,' the younger brother said. 'I will do all the travelling and the accounts.'

'Good,' said the older brother. 'I will look after the shop and the customers.'

The matter was settled in this way. The two brothers continued to look after the family business but they were no longer partners like before. They continued to work hard and the business prospered. In the course of time, the older brother and his wife had a baby boy. When the child was about ten years old, the father suddenly died.

The younger brother was grief-stricken. He could not even bring himself to comfort the sobbing wife and the child. He shut himself up in a room for many days and talked to nobody. Then finally, he told himself that he must return to work and start living again. But when he came to the shop, he found his brother's wife there, looking very unhappy.

'Now that my dear husband has died,' she said, 'I

will need his share of the family wealth to take care of my child and myself.'

'What!' shrieked the younger brother. 'Haven't you done enough? First you take away my brother and now you want to take away my money too! I'm sorry, you have no right over the family wealth.'

'But I need the money to bring up the child,' wailed his brother's wife.

'I'm sorry,' said the younger brother. 'My brother and I were no longer partners after he got married. You have to manage with what you have.'

'Then I have to seek justice at the palace,' said the woman. 'I will appeal to the king.'

'Do,' said the younger brother. 'The king will tell you exactly what I have said.'

'So, noble king, what do you say?' rasps the Vetal's voice in my ear, as I know it would. 'Do you think the woman can claim a share in the family wealth?'

'She has the right to claim a share of the wealth,' is my answer. 'After all, she got married with the consent of the younger brother, and when she married, the brothers were still business partners. So she is entitled to a share of the family property and wealth.'

'Is that what the king will say?' asks the voice.

'Yes,' I answer. 'I am sure that is what the king will say.'

'So you are sure the woman has a claim on the family wealth, is it?' the old man asked.

'Yes,' I said. 'I am sure.'

'Very good,' he told me. 'Very, very good. Your logic is unbeatable. You are truly a worthy . . .' Then his voice trailed away and I was left wondering what he was about to say and didn't.

My grandmother rushed out after lunch the next day, muttering about an important meeting with a friend. When she was at the door, she looked at me fiercely, and said, 'Why do you just sit there with a stupid look on your face? Why don't you go and search for books?' She was off even before I could open my mouth. It struck me then, dimwit that I am, that I could visit our next-door neighbour to see if she had anything on King Vikramaditya. I had been to their house once with my grandmother and seen shelves and shelves of books everywhere. It was only after I had rung the bell that I wondered whether it was the right time to visit, in the middle of the afternoon on a hot summer's day. But the old lady in her wheelchair seemed pleased to see me and said I could look around and take whatever books I wanted. 'They are my husband's collection,' she said. 'If he was alive, he would have had many stories to tell you. You would not have felt so bored then.'

How did she know I had felt bored? I was not bored any more now. Just very, very puzzled about the things that were happening to me.

She then said she was going in for her afternoon nap and all I had to do was shut the front door when I left. 'And my regards to your grandmother,' she said as she wheeled herself in. 'She is five years older than me but look how busy she keeps herself! She is remarkable.'

I looked around the room. It was full of books. They were all neatly stacked but not in any order, not like in a library. Here books on cookery jostled with books on economics, and gardening books stood side by side with huge volumes of history. How was I to look for Vikramaditya? In any case, where would I find him? Among history books or with books of fiction? Was he a real-life king or did a storyteller just make him up? Where was I to start? Then suddenly, as I looked around almost in despair, I saw something sticking out of a shelf at the far end of the room. I went up and found it was a book, all tattered and torn, with most of its pages missing. Luckily, it had a cover page with a smudged title that I could barely read. It said, *Vikram and Vetal—Stories*.

I sat down on the floor and opened the book carefully. It was so old that the paper was yellow and stiff and kept breaking up like a potato chip. Very, very carefully I turned the pages and began reading.

And here it was! Here it was, what I had been looking for. The story of Vikramaditya and the holy man who gave him fruits that became jewels. Of how the king agreed to bring the body of a dead man to the sage in return for peace and prosperity for his people. How he tramped up and down the forest, forced to listen to the stories of the Vetal, the spirit that lived in the corpse. What a villain this Vetal was! It made the king take a vow of silence and threatened to take the corpse away from him if he uttered a word. But at the end of each story, it forced Vikramaditya to answer a question. I had never heard of a more cruel thing. If the king did not speak, he would die and if he did, the Vetal would take away the corpse.

How wrong I was about Vikramaditya! He was not stupid. He was noble. Brave. He thought only of his people, not about himself. Or about pleasures. Or even comfort. And I now realized why my grandmother admired him so much. I had never heard of a king like him.

And then as I read on, I found myself trembling. Here were the stories I had heard from the strange old man in the field, and from my grandmother. The stories of the too-loyal minister, the sensitive queens, the comfort-loving king, the old man and his blind sons, of duties and rights. Here they all were and here too were the questions. The questions I was asked at the end, on what was right, and what was just.

And here were the answers.

The answers that I had given. All there. Not in absolutely the same words but nevertheless, the same thoughts. The very same answers.

'You have much more to teach the world, Vikramaditya,' screeches the voice. 'To tell the world what is right, and what is just. Come on, take the corpse on your shoulder again. Walk with it. Walk on as I tell you another story. The story of "A Noble King".'

I do not know how long I sat there on the floor with that crumbling book in my lap. The sunlight slanted across the room like bars of gold, bright and shiny. The books were all around me like pillars. Solid and familiar. And yet I felt I was floating, suspended, between forestroomkingsrightsdemonsbooksanswers. Floating. Floating . . .

The room disappeared. I smelt the forest around me and felt the tall grass against my feet. 'Today, my story is about "A Noble King",' said the voice of the old man. 'Listen to it carefully.'

A Noble King

There was once a boy in a small village who grew up hearing stories of the great and noble king who ruled the kingdom. The boy had no parents and was brought up by his grandfather who told him the stories. When the boy became a young man and was looking about for work, his grandfather died. The young man then decided that he would leave the village and go to the city to work for the noble king. 'I still have much to learn,' he said to himself, as he travelled to the city. 'And I am sure that working for a great and noble king will make me a better person.'

But when the young man reached the city, he found it was not very easy to meet the king. There were sentries at the palace gates who stopped him, there were guards at the palace doors who barred his way and there were soldiers and traders and lawyers and ministers who did not allow him anywhere close to the king. He tried to meet the king day after day, for a whole year. Anyone else might have given up but not this young man. 'I will work only for the king,' he told himself. 'And I know one day I will.'

Then on a bright spring morning, as the young man was on his daily walk to the palace, he heard that the king would not be at court that day. Instead, he was going riding in the forest with just a few attendants. The young man immediately decided to go to the forest too.

The forest was a long way off and by the time he reached there, it was dark. The young man stood at the edge of the forest, wondering what he should do. He could not see either the king or any of his attendants. Then, very faintly, he heard the sound of someone calling out for help. It seemed to be coming from inside the forest. Without a moment's thought, the young man plunged into the forest and walked quickly in the direction of the sound. It was dark, but the moon was out bright and full. The young man managed to reach a clearing in the woods, where he saw the king sitting under a tree, holding his horse by its reins and looking exhausted.

'Thank goodness,' the king said when he saw the young man. 'I didn't know whether it was a man or a wild beast coming this way. Can you help me? I am completely lost.'

'Your Majesty,' said the young man, bowing to the king. 'I am glad I heard your call for help. Here, I have some food and water. Please refresh yourself.'

'How did you know who I am?' asked the king. 'I did not wear my crown and jewels this morning and my clothes are all dusty and torn.'

'A king can always be recognized,' said the young man. 'Besides, I have been trying to meet you for a year.'

As the tired king ate the food and drank the water he was offered, the young man told him of how much he wanted to work at the palace. 'I have grown up with the stories of your greatness,' he said. 'I decided even as a boy that I would work only for you.'

The king smiled but did not say anything. When he had finished the simple meal, he lay on the ground and went to sleep while the young man stood guard over him. Early next morning, the king seated the young man behind him on the horse and rode back to the palace.

There was confusion and chaos at the palace because the attendants, who had gone to the forest with the king, had returned without him. The soldiers were shouting at the attendants, the lawyers were shouting

at the soldiers, the attendants were shouting at each
other and the ministers were shouting at everybody.
The king rode calmly into the palace courtyard on his
horse and without even raising his voice, asked for
silence.

Then he announced that he was appointing the
young man as his chief advisor. 'He will be my most
senior minister and next to me in importance,' the king
said. 'And from now on, every Tuesday and Thursday
morning, I will sit here in the palace courtyard and
meet my people. However young or old, whether rich
or poor, nobody will be stopped from meeting me.'

The young minister began his duties the same day.
He made friends with the other ministers and chatted
with the soldiers. He lunched with the lawyers and
laughed at their jokes. He bought a lot of toys from
the traders and gave them away to the children of the
sentries. By the end of the day, everybody loved him
and thought he was a fine fellow, especially the
children.

The king was very happy with his new chief advisor
and most senior minister. He found him intelligent,
hardworking and steadfast in his loyalty. In fact, the
king was so delighted that he made the young man his
dewan, the keeper of the royal treasury.

The young man was supremely happy. He had got

everything he wished for and more. Each morning he set out from his fine rooms in the palace and sat next to the king in the court, discussing matters of state. Every evening, he took a walk in the palace gardens with the king, discussing art and literature. At night, he listened to music or took a walk by himself through the streets he had got to know so well when he had spent an entire year waiting to meet the king.

It was on one of these walks along the streets of the market place that the young dewan saw somebody who stopped his breath—a beautiful girl with flowers in her hair, singing to herself as she walked. The young man walked a little behind her to find out where she lived. Next evening, he was at the door of the house that she had entered. When she came out, he went down on his knee, right there on the street, and asked her to marry him. The beautiful girl giggled and said, 'Of course I will marry you. You have such a nice voice. But please do get up. The street is dirty and you will spoil your clothes.'

The dewan and the pretty girl then took a long walk together and spoke of how beautiful the moon was, so like silver, and how the stars twinkled, so like diamonds. Then the girl said she was tired and wanted to go home. She also said, 'Please, will you come home and meet my mother tomorrow? We have to decide what I should wear for the wedding—what clothes and what jewels. You will give me lots of jewels, won't you?'

The young man promised her everything she wanted and danced his way back to the palace, singing hideously and laughing every now and then like a mad man. The king was still in the palace gardens when his dewan arrived at the gates. The king immediately understood what had happened and insisted on being told the whole story—who the girl was and where she lived. The king said that he would go with the young man the next day, and talk to the girl himself.

Next morning the young dewan was up at dawn still singing hideously as he looked through his wardrobe to choose what he should wear. Earlier, he had never really cared about what he wore, but that day he threw away set after set of his clothes, saying that none of them were good enough. Finally, the king sent him a whole set of new clothes and along with it a note that said: 'I know how you feel but please will you stop singing? All the birds in the garden have flown away and the price of earmuffs has gone up.'

When the young man was ready, he and the king set off on their horses to the house of the girl. She was waiting for them at the door, wearing fresh flowers in her hair. 'There she is,' said the excited dewan to the king as they dismounted. 'There she is. Isn't she beautiful? Isn't she stunning? Isn't she exquisite?'

When the exquisite girl saw the king and all the jewels he was wearing, she asked, 'Oh! Who is this man?'

'This is the king,' the young man replied. 'He wished to meet the woman whom I want to marry.'

Then the girl said, 'But I don't want to marry you. I want to marry the king.'

The young man was shocked. His face went white. But he controlled his feelings and stepped away from the young woman. 'Your Majesty,' he said to the king, 'This young lady chooses you over me. May I be the first to congratulate you?'

'Don't be silly,' said the king. 'You are behaving like a hero in a bad romantic story.' Then he turned to the girl and asked her, 'Young woman, yesterday you were all ready to marry this very worthy friend of mine. Why have you changed your mind today?'

'Oh,' said the young woman, 'I haven't changed my mind. It's just that I want to live in a palace and wear lots of jewels.'

'So if I give you a palace to live in and many jewels to wear, will you marry him?'

'Of course I will,' said the girl. 'He has such a nice voice.'

So the dewan and the beautiful girl were married

and they lived in a gorgeous palace where they looked as happy as the stars twinkling in the sky.

The old man's voice stopped speaking. I waited. What would be the question this time? This was a happy story, although I thought the young woman was really silly. But what was the question I would have to answer?

'Well,' the rasping voice says, 'the question this time is, who was more generous? The king? Or the young man? Answer. Answer, or I will break your head into a hundred thousand pieces.'

I thought of the young man and how much he admired the king and how grateful he was to him. Then I thought of the king and I had my answer. 'The young man was certainly generous when he stepped aside and asked the king to marry the young woman, although he himself loved her so much. But the king was even more generous. He could have easily agreed to marry the beautiful young woman. Instead, he persuaded her to marry his friend and advisor, and did all he could to make the couple happy. He was more than a king. He was also a true friend.'

'Well done!' screeches the voice. 'Well answered, great king. But alas! You have spoken and I have to return to my home with the trophy you want so much. Back I go. Back. Back. Back.'

The voice of the Vetal is ghastly as I follow it to the tamarind tree.

When I opened my eyes, there was nobody else in the room. The damp forest smell had disappeared. The walls of books stood solidly around me and the bars of sunlight were still glinting on the floor. Had the old man been here and told me another tale? The half book on my lap rustled and I found myself staring at a badly torn page on which I could just about read these words, '...man then decided that he would leave the village and go to the city to work for the noble king...'

The words were too blurred to read beyond this and when I turned the page, I found a drawing of a kingly sort of person with a moustache, carrying a hefty man's body on his shoulder. The rest of the book was missing. I got up very slowly and put the book back where I had found it. Then I tiptoed out of the room and the house, shutting the front door carefully behind me. I ran back home. I needed to think.

I climb up the stout tamarind tree again and bring down the body of the dead man. Each time I do this, I wonder who he is and why he is so important to the holy man. It is strange that there are no flies around him and no maggots are eating him. He smells, but the smell is of old decayed leaves and dead water than of rotting flesh. I would like to know who he was when he lived, but it is not my place to ask questions. I cannot ask questions. It is as if I am a child again, expected never to ask, only to obey.

'Quite right, great king,' the heavy voice is back in my ear, 'No questions from you. I ask the questions. I give the commands. It is I who am king here.' Then, in a greasy, placating way, the voice asks, 'Do you miss your authority? Do you want to go back to where you are king? Do you? Do you?'

I will not answer. I do not. 'So!' the Vetal's voice grates, 'you have given up all your kingly ways. You have sacrificed all the privileges and the comforts of being a king. And for what? For what?' Again that dreadful laughter that makes my hair stand on end. It echoes around the forest like a hundred monster jaws devouring dry wood. 'And now a story to cheer you up,' the awful voice says. 'This is a story called "The Greater Sacrifice". Sacrifice, great king, it is about sacrifice.'

I had now found out about Vikramaditya. But who was the old man? Why was he telling me these stories? How did I know the answers? And the old, torn-up book! It had the same questions! The same answers!

I had so many questions. And nobody to answer them. My grandmother was so busy she did not even have the time to give me cooking lessons. I hardly saw her. Who else was there for me to ask? My mother? She was a thousand miles away. My father was not in the country. I was alone. And I was bursting with questions.

Finally, I decided to go back to the field. After all, that was where everything started, where my summer holiday suddenly became something different. The field looked just the same, the old man was as old as he always seemed, my seat was under the tree as before, on the cool, flat stone. I sat on it and as always, suddenly, strangely, all the questions faded from my mind. It seemed as if they were not important any more.

'This is a story about generosity and sacrifice,' the old man said. 'It is called "The Greater Sacrifice".'

The Greater Sacrifice

There was once a kingdom whose king was just and generous. He had a son who was even more generous. In fact, the prince thought only of the good of the people and of how he could help others. In this good king's palace courtyard grew a peculiar tree. It was a tree that granted wishes. One day, the prince told his father that he had a plan for using the wish-granting tree. 'I would like to ask the tree to send wealth and happiness to every house in our kingdom,' he said. 'I want every man, woman and child in our kingdom to be happy and prosperous forever.'

The king was very pleased with the prince and readily agreed with the plan. As a result, all the people of the kingdom got up the next morning and found themselves very, very rich. Their kitchens were full of the most delicious food, their cupboards were bursting with clothes, and as for the gold and jewels, the ladies didn't have enough time to wear all that they had. The children were happy all day long, they played and they studied with such joy that their faces glowed and they grew big and strong.

Such happiness and prosperity cannot be hidden. Soon enough, the king's cousin, who ruled another kingdom nearby, began to feel jealous of the wealth that he saw across the border, and decided to wage war against his cousin. The prince felt very sad when he heard of this. He told his father, 'Let us not have war and bloodshed. Let my uncle take over the kingdom. In any case, our people will always be happy and prosperous.'

The king too was clear that he did not want bloodshed. 'But we still have to live our lives,' he told the prince. 'If we give up the kingdom, where do we go and what do we do?'

The prince smiled. 'At the borders of our kingdom,' he said, 'there is a mountain range. Across the mountains, on the other side, is a beautiful, wooded valley. I think we could live there like the hill people do. We could build a small hut and have a farm with goats and cows and chickens. It won't be a kingly life but it will be peaceful and calm.'

The king agreed and soon they made their way to

the valley. The air was crisp and clean and their cheeks were brushed by a soft, sweet-smelling breeze. When they reached a sparkling little mountain stream, the prince said, 'I think this is where we should build ourselves a small hut.'

In a few days, the hut was ready and the king, queen and prince set up home. They bought cows and goats and chickens. Soon they had enough milk for themselves and sold the rest to the hill people who also came to them for eggs and vegetables. The royal family was well settled and happy. The king and the queen lost all their aches and pains and began to look younger with each passing day. As for the prince, he whistled as he woke up and he whistled while he worked. He sang when he milked the cows and sang as he brought the goats home. Never was there a happier prince.

One day, as he was walking along the valley, he saw a beautiful girl by the banks of the stream gathering flowers. He liked her so much that he ran to his father and said, 'Father! I have never seen a sweeter girl in my life. Please find out who she is. I want to marry her.'

The king was very happy to see the prince so excited. He asked the hill people about the girl and was told that she was the daughter of a holy man who lived on the other side of the stream. The king and the queen went to meet him and were received with great affection. The wedding took place almost immediately after. The prince was happier than ever before.

One day, as he was bringing the goats home, he found that a baby goat had wandered some distance away and was caught in a prickly bush. He went whistling up to rescue it and saw something ghastly. On the other side of the prickly bush was a small hill, on top of which was a huge heap of human bones, picked clean. The prince was overcome with sorrow. 'Who is it that has killed so many people?' he asked himself. 'I have to find the killer and stop him.'

So the prince sent the little goat back to its mother and stood waiting by the bush. 'The killer will come,' he told himself, 'he will come here, sooner or later.'

As the sun was about to set, the prince heard the sound of wailing. He saw a woman with a young boy coming towards the bush. 'My poor son!' the woman wailed, 'My only son! And I have to give him up! How can I bear it? How can I bear it?'

The prince stepped up to the woman and asked her what the matter was. Through her tears, the woman said, 'Kind sir, there is a cruel eagle here who is an enemy of our tribe. Every day, he demands the body of a male of our tribe for his food. If we don't give him what he wants, he will destroy all of us. Today it is the turn of my little boy to be killed.'

The prince was aghast. 'Where is the chief of your tribe?' he asked angrily. 'Why does he not kill the eagle?'

The woman wept fresh tears. 'Sir, our chief is weak and afraid,' she said. 'It was he who decided that to keep the eagle happy we must give up a male person from our households, turn by turn.'

'No!' thundered the prince. 'I will not let this happen. You go home with your son. I will face this cruel eagle.'

As the prince finished speaking, there was the sound of a huge, vast bird flying towards them. The woman shrieked and hid her son behind her. The eagle swept down, picked up the prince and flew up to the top of the small hill. Once there, it began to rip open the body of the prince. His blood-soaked ring flew off his finger and landed near the door of his hut. The princess saw it and realized that something terrible had happened. She ran along the path that the goats usually took and saw, across the bush, the cruel sight of her prince being torn apart by an enormous eagle.

She also saw something else. A young boy was running towards the eagle, shouting, 'No, do not kill him. Let him go. He is not of our tribe. I am the one you have to eat.'

Then she heard her prince say, even as he was dying, 'Let my death bring peace to the world.'

When the eagle heard these words, it dropped the prince from its beak. It realized that this was no ordinary

person. At the same time, the princess came running up the hill, pleading with the eagle to let go her husband. But she was too late. Her prince was already dead.

'A very sad story, a really sad story,' murmurs the voice of the Vetal, in totally insincere tones. 'But tell me,' the voice grates after a pause, 'whose sacrifice was greater? Who was the more noble person? The prince who gave up his life for a tribe he did not even know? Or the little boy who offered his? Answer, great king. Give me your answer or I will break your head into a thousand pieces.'

The old man's voice was stern. 'Yes, it is a sad story,' he said. 'But my question is, who was the more noble of the two? Who made the greater sacrifice?'

I thought again of the ghastly scene on the hilltop, the sobbing mother, her little son bravely facing the eagle, the princess crying, bending over the mangled body of her prince, and towering above them all the massive bird with its sharp, cruel beak. 'It was the young boy who was the more noble person,' I said. 'The prince was always noble, always generous. But that small boy! How frightened he must have been! How his mother must have tried to hold him back! And yet, he broke away from her and ran up to the eagle offering to be killed. That calls for enormous courage.'

The old man's voice was gentle now. 'You are absolutely right,' he said. 'It was the little boy who was the nobler one.'

Then after a moment, the old man said, 'But the story has a happy ending. The princess prayed to the gods to give back the life of her prince and the gods were so moved by her tears that they did. When the prince stood up tall and well again, he made the eagle promise not to hurt the tribespeople ever again. And finally, the eagle was so amazed at all that had happened, that it used its magical powers and brought back to life all the tribesmen that it had killed.'

'Thank goodness,' I said as I wiped away the tears that were suddenly in my eyes. I thought I heard the old man chuckle, but when I looked up to see him, he was gone.

The Vetal's voice crackles hideously. 'You are right great king,' it says in my ear. 'The boy was the nobler of the two. Yes, the frightened little boy made the greater sacrifice. And yet, the story does not end here. Do you want to know the end, noble king? Do you?'

I do not answer. The rasping voice is already high above me, drawing the corpse with it, and I follow the voice, as it tells the end of the story. The happy end.

As I went back home, I thought about Vikramaditya. He was not just noble, he was also smart, clever. Each time I heard a story, I realized how important it was to be intelligent. Not just that. One has to use one's intelligence too, and not let it sit like a stone in one's head. There were so many people I knew, my friends, their parents, even some of the teachers in school, who made me feel that they had not used their brains for a long time, as if their intelligence lay inside them like a large heap of tamarind, souring.

The lights were all ablaze when I reached home. It looked like a wedding house. I also realized that it was darker than usual and there was a smell in the air, as if there were a lot of wet clothes around. I found my grandmother at home, speaking excitedly into the phone, about somebody coming on a visit. When she finished, she turned to me with a huge smile and said,

'Manu will be here tomorrow. This time tomorrow he will be here.'

'Manu?' I asked.

'Your cousin Manu,' she said a little impatiently. 'Your second cousin actually, since he is my sister's son. Don't you remember him? He used to be here with all you children during the summer holidays.'

And then I remembered. Manu! Of course! The tall cousin with the bad leg who looked more like an uncle than a cousin. He never played any games. We used to call him Man and behind his back, Ma or even Lame Ma, because he scolded us if we made a noise or talked rudely to anybody. They used to make me call out funny names to him from outside his window and then run away. 'He might catch you but he won't scold you,' they said, 'because you are still a kid.' Man never scolded me but he used to look quite angry.

I did not understand why my grandmother was so excited about his visit. She was darting about now picking up files and papers and books. 'I have to get things absolutely ready before he arrives,' she said. 'He won't have much time, poor fellow. These young lawyers work so hard. But it is a good sign, a very good sign. It shows that people are becoming aware of the legal system and of the laws that can help them.'

I wondered if Man, the lawyer, would talk to me.

Would he have heard of Vikramaditya? Would I be able to ask him all those questions that were still pinching my mind? Would I be able to tell him of the old man? Would he laugh at me if I did, and think that I had dreamt it all?

My grandmother was still on the phone, still talking excitedly, when I went to sleep. Next day, she was very busy getting things ready for Manu and did not even notice when I slipped out of the house in the middle of the day and wandered out. There were clouds in the sky, small busy clouds that seemed to be in a hurry to go somewhere else. They reminded me of my grandmother. And my mother. And all those people who did not have time for me.

Then I suddenly stopped and stared. Was I seeing right? Was it the old man in the field? But this was morning, not our usual afternoon story time. Yet he was there, the old, old man smelling a bit peculiar, his face turned away. 'Sit,' he said, without looking up. 'Today my story is called "The Talented Brothers".'

I was about to say that he had already told me the story of the two brothers who were blind but highly talented, when he said, 'Do not ask me any questions or argue with me. The story I am about to tell you is not about blind men. Just listen.'

I am back with my smelly burden, my 'trophy' as the Vetal refers to it. I slash my way through as I have done so many times now. Is there any end to this?

'Not yet! Not yet!' the voice mocks me. 'There is still so much wisdom I need to learn from you. So much!' The laugh is like the howling of mad wolves. 'Today,' the voice says, 'my story is called "The Talented Brothers".'

I dare not tell the Vetal that he has already told me the story. I remember it well. It is about two blind but unusually talented brothers.

The voice howls with laughter. 'No!' it says. 'This is not about blind men. Listen, and do not open your mouth. Do not say a word.'

The Talented Brothers

There was once a king, who had in his palace two very talented brothers. The older of the two could tell what a person was thinking and what kind of a person he was, by merely looking at the face. The younger brother had to only touch or smell something, however strange the thing may be, and say what it was and where it came from.

The king often asked them to help him whenever there were disputes that seemed impossible to solve. Once, two men came to his court quarrelling violently over an expensive pearl necklace. One man was tall with a long nose and the other was short with a heavy jaw. They both claimed the necklace was their property and that the other man had stolen it.

'I was carrying the necklace from my mother to my wife,' said the tall man, 'when this man pushed past me in the street. When I looked in my bag a moment later, the necklace was gone.'

'Nonsense!' spluttered the short, heavy-jawed man. 'The necklace is mine. I was taking it to the jeweller to have it cleaned, when this man pushed past me in the street.'

The two men fought so loudly and so long and the short man spluttered so much that the king got a headache. He sent for the two talented brothers and asked them for their advice. The older brother looked at the two men while the younger held the necklace and smelt it. Then they both leaned across and whispered into the king's ears, one into the left ear and the other into the right, that the necklace belonged to the short man with the heavy jaw.

When the king said, 'I am sure the necklace belongs to the short man,' the tall man with the long nose fell at the king's feet and begged forgiveness. 'Your Majesty, you are right. The necklace is his, not mine. Please, please forgive me. It was I who pushed past him on the street and stole the necklace.'

After this, the king decided that he would ask the two brothers to be present at court every day. 'I should have done this much earlier,' the king said. 'It would have saved me a great many headaches.'

With the help of the two brothers, the king was

able to bring peace to his kingdom. Disputes were quickly resolved. The innocent were protected, the guilty were found out and punished. With peace came prosperity and the kingdom flourished as never before. The king's headaches vanished and he began to travel outside his kingdom to meet other kings and enjoy their hospitality. But wherever he went, he took the two brothers with him. 'A king can never be too trusting,' he told himself. 'One never quite knows when friendship ends and enmity begins.'

It so happened that the king of the neighbouring kingdom sent out a very warm invitation to a three-day grand festival in his palace. 'It is the end of summer,' the invitation said, 'and the start of the monsoon, when the earth wakes up to freshness and joy. We would like you to welcome the rain with us and dance and sing.'

Our king, the hero of the story, asked the two brothers what they thought of the invitation. The younger brother smelt the invitation letter and said, 'The king who sent this to you is a good person, Your Majesty, but you have to be careful of him because he is a little jealous of you.'

The king decided to accept the invitation and set out to the neighbouring kingdom. The two brothers accompanied him. On the way, the king told them to look out for anything unusual or dangerous. 'I am not sure what our host plans to do,' said the king. 'It may all be fine. On the other hand, there may be some attempt to harm me.'

The host received his royal guest very warmly. 'I have arranged for a huge banquet tonight,' he said, 'and then, good neighbour, we will celebrate the monsoon season tomorrow.' Our king sat at the banquet table with the two brothers on either side of him. The food was rich and delicious but he did not eat anything till the younger brother had tasted it and found it safe. When the feast was over, he was shown to a beautiful room with a large and comfortable bed.

'I am so tired,' the king said, sitting on the edge of the bed, 'I have been wanting to lie down and sleep for the last half an hour.'

'Stop!' the older brother said suddenly. 'Stop, Your Majesty. Do not lie down please. There is something wrong with the pillow. It is dangerous.'

Immediately, the younger brother stepped forward and picked up the pillow. He felt it all over and smelt it. 'My brother is right, Your Majesty,' he said. 'This pillow is a death trap.'

'A pillow, a death trap?' asked the king. 'What do you mean?'

'Look, Your Majesty,' said the younger brother. He ripped open the pillow. In the middle of the soft, fluffy cotton was a single strand of hair, like a long and thick needle. 'This is animal hair,' said the younger brother, 'And it is smeared with poison. It would have gone through the cotton and pierced your neck as you slept.'

The king was shocked and very, very angry. 'I do not want to be here another minute,' he said. 'Let us return to our kingdom.' And so, in the middle of the night, although it was dark and raining, the king left for home. He did not even meet his host before he left. 'Let him think I am dead,' he said. 'Tomorrow, he will know that I know what he had planned.'

The king brought the dangerous pillow home with him and had it examined by his royal chemist who told him exactly what the two brothers had said and in almost the same words. 'This pillow is a death trap, Your Majesty,' said the royal chemist. 'If the hair in it had even touched human skin, it would have caused instant death.'

'So the king's life was saved,' said the old man, 'but my question is, which of the two brothers was the more talented and the wiser one? The younger brother? Or the older brother?'

I did not need much time to think, 'The older

brother was the wiser one,' I said. 'The younger had to touch an object and smell it before he could say anything about it. But the older brother could judge people or things just by looking at them.'

'Absolutely right,' said the old man. 'You are absolutely right.'

'Also,' I went on, 'if the older brother had not felt the pillow was dangerous as soon as he looked at it, the king might very well have died. Who would think of ripping open a pillow to see if it was safe?'

There was a moment's silence. Then the old man said, 'You are certainly very wise, great king. I salute you.'

Great king! Had he said great king? I opened my eyes with a start, but he was gone.

'You are absolutely right as always,' screeches the voice in my ear. 'Of course the king would have died if the older brother had not sensed that the pillow was dangerous. You are certainly wise, great king. I salute you.'

I do not need the Vetal's salutations. I merely want to deliver this corpse to the holy man. That is all.

'Not yet, not yet,' shrieks the hateful voice now high above me. 'I have taken away your precious dead man. I have whisked him away.'

I turn around and walk back to the tamarind tree.

My grandmother's house was full of noise and people. There were cars all along the road on both sides and bicycles inside the driveway. I had to squeeze past them to get into the house. There were people at the gate and people waiting at the door and people sitting inside. My grandmother was at the dining table which was covered with papers and books and files and surrounded by more people. She looked up and caught sight of me. 'Manu arrived early,' she shouted over the din. 'You have to eat in the kitchen.'

The man sitting next to her waved cheerfully and gave me a big smile. Manu! Man! I recognized him though he now wore glasses and looked a bit different. But he smiled. The Man I remembered hardly ever smiled.

I ate in the kitchen where there wasn't even a chair to sit on. I felt very left out. I wondered whether I should go back to my field, to my umbrella tree, and to my cool stone seat. I looked out through the back door and saw more dark clouds scudding about. The wind was picking up and I heard a door slamming somewhere down the street.

'You don't have to feel so sorry for yourself,' laughed a voice behind me. I whirled around. It was Man. Not as tall as I remembered and quite thin. He was smiling.

'You never used to smile so much,' I said, and then felt very stupid. 'Hello,' I added.

He swung himself up awkwardly and sat on the kitchen counter. I tried not to look at his bad leg and its heavy, ugly shoe.

'I was afraid to smile,' he said. 'You kids were pretty cruel. Do you remember the names everybody called me?'

'Sort of,' I had to say. I felt terrible. 'Do you want to eat?' I asked. 'There is a lot of food.'

'I was sent here to eat,' he said. 'But I'm not hungry. I ate on my way here.'

There was silence. I still felt terrible. 'So what is it like to be a famous lawyer?' I asked.

'Your grandmother exaggerates,' he said. 'I've only just started working. But I like law and I like to help people if I can.'

'Is that what you have come for?' I asked. 'To help people?'

He looked surprised. 'I have come to help your grandmother with her work,' he said.

'What work?'

'Don't you know what your grandmother does?' he asked.

'Well,' I told him. 'She writes a lot of letters and talks on the phone and if she has the time, she tries to teach me to cook.'

He laughed. It was not a jokey laugh. 'You sound just as spoilt as I always thought you were,' he said.

Spoilt? Me? Nobody had ever called me spoilt before. I was about to fling myself out of the kitchen when he stopped me. 'All those people will see you crying,' he said. 'Wash your face before you go.'

'I won't,' I said angrily. But I stayed. I did not want any nosey person to ask why I was crying.

'Your grandmother,' he said, as if nothing had happened, 'is trying to help people get justice. There are a lot of people in our country who are too poor or not educated enough to know how the law can help them. Many of them are women. Your grandmother meets these people, listens to their stories and does what she can for them.'

'But she is not a lawyer,' I said.

'That's true,' he answered. 'She is not legally trained. But she can always find lawyers who will help her. Like me. But what she does have is a very great sense of justice. She knows what is right and what is not. That is a remarkable gift to have.'

'Why is it remarkable?' I asked.

'Because,' he said, 'most people have very mixed-up feelings about money and property and about how to live with each other. Justice has nothing to do with feelings. Justice has to do with rights and duties, with correctness. Your grandmother is able to separate what is correct from what is not.'

'So she does not have feelings?' I asked.

He smiled. 'No, that's not what I meant,' he said. 'Everybody has feelings. So does your grandmother. That is how we are human. But she is able to see that the other person also has feelings. So she is very fair in what she thinks. And most important, she uses her brains, her intelligence, to deal with feelings.'

He paused. Then in a different tone of voice he said, 'I'm sorry about that comment I made. I should have remembered that in this same house, many years ago, I used to feel so very sorry for myself. I hated all of you for being healthy, for having two sturdy legs. What did I have? One and a half legs. I was a freak. I used to watch all of you playing and I would wish . . . well I wished terrible things.'

He stopped. I did not know what to say. Then he went on, 'It was your grandmother who got me out of it. She told me a story.'

'A story?'

'Yes. A weird story. But I still remember every word of it. It has a lot of gruesome things like beheadings. Do you want to hear it?'

'Yes please,' I said. And then I added, 'I'm sorry for all those names we used to call you.'

He smiled then. 'Just listen to the story,' he said. 'And don't speak till I have finished. The story is called "A Difficult Decision".'

'Just one more story, great king,' the voice screeches. 'Just one more. Yes, I know you do not trust me. But remember, I hold your life in my hands.'

I know that. I can fight and win over any mortal being. But how do I fight that which I cannot see, this thing without a form; this thing that cannot even die? The voice screeches louder. 'You cannot vanquish me, great king, you have to do what I say. Keep your mouth shut when I tell you. Speak when I demand it.' The hideous laugh echoes through the forest. 'Now listen,' the voice says, 'Listen to this story called "A Difficult Decision".'

A Difficult Decision

There was once a handsome prince whose best friend was a washerman's son. The prince's father, the king, believed that everybody is equal, whether they are born in a palace or in a hut. So he sent his son to an ordinary school and made sure that the washerman's son was given riding lessons with the prince. The two friends visited each other every day and took long walks together, discussing life and books and art and what they would do when they were older. They also talked about girls, as all young men do.

'I want to marry a sweet, beautiful girl,' said the prince. 'I don't care if she is not a princess. I just want a sweet beautiful girl.'

The washerman's son did not say anything. He was already in love with his neighbour's daughter who he thought was the sweetest, most beautiful girl in the world. He met her every day and talked to her, but he had not spoken of his love for her. For some reason, he felt very shy about it. He had not even told his best friend, the prince, about his feelings.

Then one day, as the two friends were walking along the river bank, the prince stopped suddenly and said, 'I have found her! I have found the sweetest, most beautiful girl in the world. Look!' And he pointed to a young woman who was walking on the other side of the river, with a heavy load of washing on her head.

The heart of the washerman's son went cold. The prince was pointing to his neighbour's daughter, the girl he loved. But he said nothing.

'I have to meet her, I have to talk to her,' said the prince all excited. 'Come, let us run and catch up with her. Come on!'

Then the washerman's son spoke. 'There is no hurry,' he said. 'I know where she lives. She is our neighbour's daughter.'

So with the help of his friend, the prince met the beautiful girl and grew to love her more and more every day. Finally, one day, he went to his father and told him he wanted to marry the daughter of a washerman.

'You have always said that all those born in the world are equal,' he said. 'So give me permission to marry this beautiful girl.'

The king did not know what to do. It was true that he thought everyone in the world are equal. He had not stopped his son from being friends with a washerman's son. But when it came to the prince marrying a washerman's daughter, he was not sure.

Finally, the king said, 'I have no objection. But son, since your mother is no more, I do not know anyone whose advice I can take. Do bear with me. Do not be in a hurry, I beg you. Wait a little before you rush into marriage.'

The prince was heartbroken. He knew what the king was thinking. He was hoping that if he waited, the prince would lose his interest in the girl. 'That will never happen,' the prince told himself. That night, the prince slipped out of the palace and went to the temple of the Dark Goddess, up on a hilltop. He prayed to the goddess to help him marry the girl he loved. 'If you help me, Goddess,' he said, 'I promise to cut off my head here in your temple on the next full moon night after my wedding.'

There was a huge clap of thunder when he finished speaking, as if the goddess had heard his prayer.

The prince returned to the palace and after that, refused to go out anywhere. He sat in his room by the window, looking out at the river, not eating, not meeting anybody. His best friend did all he could to bring him out of his misery but the prince merely turned his face away and would not listen. As the days went by, the prince became thinner and thinner. He now lay in bed all day staring at the ceiling. Finally, one day, the washerman's son went to the king and said, 'Your Majesty, I think the life of the prince is in danger. He has refused to eat these last many days. He has grown so thin and weak, I am frightened.'

The king, who had been very busy with the affairs of his kingdom, was shocked when he saw his son. He immediately told the prince that he could marry the washerman's daughter. The prince jumped up with joy when he heard this. He hugged his father and his friend and wanted to rush off at once to see the girl. But he was persuaded to eat and have a bath and change his clothes before going out.

'You have grown so weak and thin,' said his friend. 'You should be careful.'

It is remarkable what happiness can do. In a very few days, the prince was back to his normal, cheerful self and getting ready for his wedding, bustling about, ordering new clothes, buying jewellery, talking, laughing, singing. The wedding was a grand affair. The best musicians had been called, the most fragrant flowers had been ordered from around the kingdom and the food had been cooked by the most skilled cooks ever to be found.

In all the merriment and joy, there was only one sore heart and that belonged to the washerman's son. But he hid his feelings well and nobody noticed, certainly not the prince.

After the wedding, the prince and his bride moved to the new palace that the king had built for them. The prince was now completely happy. He wanted nothing more than to spend the day riding or walking about with his new bride and his best friend. They talked and they sang and they made up ridiculous games. The prince was so happy that he hardly realized how the days went by and the next full moon night after the wedding had already arrived.

That night, the prince told his bride and his friend that he had a special plan. 'I want to go to the temple of the Dark Goddess,' he said.

'Now? At night?' asked the princess.

'Yes, my dearest,' said the prince with a smile. 'It is at night that one goes to the temple of the Dark Goddess.'

So after the evening meal, the prince, his bride and his best friend went up the hill to the temple of the Dark Goddess. The moon hung over them like a silver plate, a huge medallion.

'How beautiful the moon is,' said the young bride.

'Not as beautiful as you,' said the prince and held his bride close.

The washerman's son turned away and tried to keep his eyes dry.

'Come here you,' said the prince to his friend, with rough tenderness, 'come here and give me a hug too.'

When they reached the temple, the prince asked his bride and his friend to wait outside. 'I want to be alone with the goddess for a minute,' he said and disappeared into the temple. But when he did not reappear after more than ten minutes, they got alarmed. 'You wait here,' said the washerman's son to the prince's bride, 'Let me go in and see what has happened to the prince.'

When the washerman's son went into the temple, he saw a horrible sight. The head of the prince lay separated from the body in a pool of blood. 'No!' cried the prince's best friend. 'You cannot leave me like this.' And he too beheaded himself.

The young bride waiting outside heard the terrible cry and she rushed into the temple too. What a ghastly scene she saw! The heads of her prince and of his best friend lay separated from their bodies and there was blood everywhere. The young bride wailed with terror and sorrow. 'Oh Goddess!' she called out. 'What have you done? Why have you done this? What will become of me?' And in her great sorrow, the young girl fell to the ground and died.

The Dark Goddess was much moved by what had happened. She saw how the prince had kept his promise to her, the loyalty of the prince's friend who died for him, and the sorrow of his young bride. The goddess decided to restore life to all three of them. Suddenly, there was a huge clap of thunder and the prince, his bride and his best friend rose to their feet, as if they had been merely asleep and were now awake.

'So, is that the end of the story?' I asked Man. 'Is there a question?'

My cousin threw a curious look at me and said, 'No. That is not the end of the story. But how did you know there is a question? Did you know it is a Vikram–Vetal story?'

'I guessed,' I told him.

'But that is not the end of the story,' the voice cackles

in my ear. 'Did you think it was the end, great king, did you?'

There was a huge clap of thunder, and the prince, his bride and his best friend, rose to their feet, as if they had been merely asleep and were now awake. They remembered nothing of what had happened. But as they got ready to leave the temple, the Dark Goddess realized that she had made a terrible mistake. When giving them life, she had mixed up the heads of the two friends, so that now the prince's body carried the head of the washerman's son and the head of the prince was attached to the body of his best friend.

'What have I done? Who is the husband of that young woman now?' asked the goddess to herself. And then she thought, 'These humans are capable of finding a solution to the problem. What is done is done.'

'My question,' screeches the Vetal, 'is the one that the goddess asked herself. Who is now the husband of the young woman? Is it the man who has the head of the prince and the body of the washerman's son? Or is it the man who has the head of the washerman's son and the body of the prince? Which is the right man, noble king, which one?'

I looked at Man in dismay. 'I don't know the answer,' I whispered. 'The two men are now half of one and half of the other. How can I answer this question?'

Man's voice was gentle. 'I couldn't either,' he said. 'It was your grandmother who gave me the answer.'

I have the answer. It is simple. 'The true husband is the man who carries the head of the prince. It is the head that controls the body. It is the head, the brains of a person that determines the character and behaviour of that person. And so, the man with the head of the prince is the true husband of the young woman.'

'It is the head that controls a person, after all. And so I realized that my disability did not matter,' said Man. 'I had the head, the brains to make something of myself. And now people do not even realize that I have a bad leg.'

I made up my mind quickly. 'Can you come out with me?' I asked. 'Does my grandmother want you now?'

'Not for the moment,' he said, a little surprised. 'I think I can safely be away for half an hour or so without being missed.'

'Then come with me. I want to show you something,' I said.

We went out through the back door. Man did not need crutches but I had to slow down for him. I wanted to run, to fly to my field but I wanted Man to be with me too. We crossed the colony to the road leading to the fields. There were no houses here, only open spaces and fields.

'Do you come here all by yourself?' asked Man.

'Yes I do,' I said. 'There's nothing to be afraid of. Except some scared grass snakes.'

And then, as we were halfway there, the rain came down. Suddenly. Hugely. Enormously. It exploded over us as if a hundred thousand tankers of water had burst in the heavens, all at the same time. It came down with a thunderous beat, like the trumpeting of gigantic elephants.

'What do we do now?' I shouted to Man.

'Get wet,' he shouted back, with a laugh.

We carried on. The rain streamed down our faces and into our eyes and noses. It came down in curtains, shutting us off from the narrow pavement and the ditch beyond. I could not see anything except the tip of my very wet nose.

'We better walk in the middle of the road,' yelled Man.

'Where is the middle?' I yelled back.

'Hold my hand,' he shouted.

'Where is your hand?' I shouted back.

We staggered along like drunken people, shouting to each other and laughing for no good reason. We slipped and slithered and I held on to Man's hand as the ground dissolved beneath our feet and little rivulets of water formed all around us.

'They are predicting a good monsoon this year,' shouted Man.

'Good!' I shouted back. 'I can see it.'

And then there was a sudden thinning of the rain, like a small clearing in a thick, dense forest. We were at the field, my field. I stopped. There it was, my umbrella tree, blurred, swaying in the rain and there . . . No. He wasn't there. There was no old man. There was no old man there at all.

'What is it?' Manu asked, coming up from behind. 'What are you looking for?'

'Nothing,' I said. 'There's nothing here. Let's go back home.'

The Vetal

That night I dreamt of King Vikramaditya. I dreamt I was King Vikramaditya.

The forest was dark and smelly and the dead man on my shoulder stank. I had gone up the tree to fetch him down many, many times and now I wondered how many more times I would have to do it.

'Excellent answer,' screeched a voice in my ear. 'Yes, great king, it is the head that rules the body. You have answered correctly and now it is time for me to free you.'

I said nothing. I walked on. How could I trust the Vetal? Even in the freedom that I was promised, there might be danger, something else that I had to be alert about.

'Trust me,' the voice of the Vetal pierced through my ear. 'You are free to go to your holy man now. You are free to carry your trophy to him.'

Was I really free? This thing, this Vetal that had tormented me, that was outside life, death and outside time itself, how could I trust it?

'But I am still here, great king,' hissed the voice in my ear. 'See! I have not returned to my dear tamarind tree. You broke your vow of silence and yet I remain. I am here.'

I could now see the edge of the forest. I ran towards it with the body of the dead man swinging wildly on my shoulder. I did not want the Vetal to take away the corpse just as I reached the end of my journey. At the edge of the forest, like a small dot, I saw the hut of the holy man and the thin tendrils of smoke from his fire. 'Stop!' screamed the Vetal suddenly. 'Stop.'

I stopped. What was it now?

'It is time for me to warn you,' said the hateful voice. 'This holy man you are about to meet is a wicked man. He is evil.'

Evil? How was he evil? How could he be more evil than you? 'Believe me,' rasped the Vetal. 'He wants to destroy you. He will ask you to bow to him so that he can give his blessings. But when you do and the back of your neck is unprotected, he will slash your head off your shoulder, just as your sword slashed through the nooses of the forest. I warn you. Beware

of him, great king, beware.'

I did not wait to hear any more. I ran quickly to the holy man standing by the fire, and flung the corpse at his feet. He seemed pleased to see me. 'Now I can finish my work, thanks to you, mighty king,' he said. He picked up the dead man's body by its head, and threw it into the fire. The fire hissed and spat huge green-blue sparks. 'Come, mighty king,' said the holy man. 'Come, let me bless you. Let me bless you with prosperity and good fortune for all time to come.'

'But I don't want anything for myself,' I said in my dream. 'I have done this for my people. So that they may be prosperous and enjoy peace for all time.'

His eyes glinted. 'That was what I meant,' he said. 'Come, stand before me. Take my blessings. Come on. Do not waste my time.'

I was a king. I did not trust easily. I saw something in his eyes that gave me warning. 'I am a king,' I told him. 'I do not bow to anyone, except to my god and my parents.'

My sword was ready to leap as he turned at me with madness in his hands. He moved towards me but my sword was quicker—quicker than a thought. He crumpled and fell at my feet. Dead.

'Ha! Ha! Ha!' laughed a voice. 'Aren't you glad I warned you?'

I whirled around. Vetal?

'Don't you recognize me?' the voice continued. 'Look! You have given me life again, great and noble king.'

And there, in front of me stood an old man, wearing the white robes of a sage. He looked astonishingly like the man who now lay dead at my feet.

Was this another trick?

'Who are you?' I asked.

'I am the brother of this evil man who lies dead here,' said the old man. 'He had a powerful mind and learnt many great and wonderful skills. But alas! He turned to wicked ways. He wanted more and more power. He wanted to gain control over all mankind. He believed that if he killed two kings who shared his birthday and time of birth, he would get what he wanted—supreme power.

'So he searched for two such kings and he found them. One was the man whose body you carried through the forest. My brother murdered him. When I wanted to stop him, my brother tried to kill me too.'

'What did you do?' I asked.

'I also have some powers,' the old man replied. 'I turned myself into a Vetal. I was invisible and I was a spirit between life and death. My brother could not do anything to me. How can you kill something that has no life? I was safe from my brother, but I could not return to life without the help of somebody noble. I waited. My brother had hung the corpse of the king on that tamarind tree in the forest. I stayed inside the body because I knew my brother would need it for his final ritual. He knew where I was, but he also knew I would trap him if he came to the forest. So he made you fetch the corpse.'

'Then why did he attack me?' I asked. 'I gave him what he wanted. I brought him the body of the dead king. And with it, the brother he hated and feared. Then why did he want to kill me too?'

The old man is silent for a moment. Then he answers. 'Because you are the other king who shared his birthday and time of birth, Vikramaditya. He had to kill you too. Only then would he become the most powerful man in the universe.'

I cannot understand this, this devouring greed for power. This greed that made a learned man a murderer, a criminal who could attack even his own brother.

Then I remember that there is something else I need to know.

'Why did you trouble me so much?' I ask. 'Why did you make me take a vow of silence and then force me to break it each time you finished a story? And why did you insist on telling me all those stories?'

The old man smiles. 'I was not sure of you,' he says. 'I was not sure whether my brother had gained control over you as well. So I tested you with stories and questions that only a wise man can answer, one with a keen sense of justice.' He smiles again. 'And each time you came through magnificently. You truly are a noble king.'

The old man pauses. Then, almost in a whisper, he says, 'You have released me from my prison. It was agony to live as a Vetal in that poor king's body, to be a stranger to the rhythm of time, to hang forever between life and death. To not be completely alive, nor completely dead.'

Then, in a stronger voice he says, 'Great king! Tell me how I can repay you. Ask for anything you want. I have the power to fulfil it.'

I am silent for a moment. Then I tell him, 'I want nothing for myself. But those stories you narrated to me are very valuable to humankind. May I ask that they be remembered for all time to come?'

'They shall be remembered,' declares the old man. His face creases into a thousand smiles. How could I have thought him evil? 'They shall be remembered across history, through time, as the Vikram–Vetal stories. They shall be told in school rooms, in the halls of law, in marketplaces. They shall be heard where great leaders meet to discuss peace, wherever men and women look for justice.'

Then he says, very softly, 'And they shall be told to a child, sitting under a tamarind tree, alone in a dusty field.'

I woke up with a start. The sun was shining brightly. The storm was over. My grandmother was fussing over Man at the dining table. 'Really, you two gave me palpitations yesterday,' she scolded. 'How did you think you would survive that kind of a cloudburst?'

Man grinned at me. 'We have a baby cousin,' he said. 'She was born last night, right in the middle of the storm. Yes,' he continued, even before I could ask. 'The monsoon has broken all over the country. In much the same way. And many people were scolded by their grandmothers.'

Later, when the house filled up with people again and Man and my grandmother got busy with their work, I ran out towards the field, my field. The air smelt fresh and newly washed and the road was shining clean. The ditches on both sides of the road looked like rivers, merrily flowing to some unseen, sparkling sea. Everywhere people were smiling, waving to me, talking cheerfully to one another. The summer was over.

And then I saw the tamarind tree. It was standing deep in water, with its branches outspread like the spokes of a very wet umbrella. I looked around but there was nobody, anywhere. No one covered in a black robe, sitting still as if he was watching a serene blue sea where sailboats skimmed and dipped like dancers on ice skates. The field was empty. And completely flooded. I waded in and the water came up to my knees, my feet slithered in thick, swirling mud. I looked for my stone seat, the throne. I could not find it.

I put my arms around the tree and looked up into its shadowed canopy, dense with branch and leaf and things damp. I smelt the forest again. I closed my eyes as I had done so often before, sitting under this tree, and wafted back into the lives of princesses and kings and warriors, into the stories of people I had never met. But they were no longer strangers; they were my friends now, they had helped me grow up. I would remember them forever.

Then I thought I heard his voice. My heart jumped, I opened my eyes and looked across to where he usually sat. There was nobody there. Nobody at all. But in the distance, far away on the rainswept horizon, I saw a strange, solitary cloud. It looked like an ancient black robe flung up against the sky.